SAM

SAM

BARBARA CORCORAN

DRAWINGS BY BARBARA MCGEE

Atheneum 1967 New York

For Jeanne

Poem "Silver" by Walter de la Mare quoted by permission of The Literary Trustees of Walter de la Mare and The Society of Authors as their representative.

SPRING AND FALL
TO A YOUNG CHILD

Margaret, are you grieving
Over Goldengrove unleaving?
Leaves, like the things of man, you
With your fresh thoughts care for, can you?
Ah! as the heart grows older
It will come to such sights colder
By and by, nor spare a sigh
Though worlds of wanwood leafmeal lie;
And yet you will weep and know why,
Now no matter, child, the name:
Sorrow's springs are the same.
Nor mouth had, no nor mind, expressed
What heart heard of, ghost guessed:
It is the blight man was born for,
It is Margaret you mourn for.

GERALD MANLEY HOPKINS

Until today it had not disturbed her that her first name, legally inscribed on her birth certificate, was Sam. Last winter when her father finally sent her to school, the teachers thought it was a nickname. But she was used to that, and she had stopped explaining that her father had expected a boy. Today, though, when the music teacher said, "How did you ever come by a name like that?" Sam had felt ridiculous.

"Somebody's coming," Mark said. The maze of wires and gadgets at his elbow whirred faintly, like a rattler about to strike. Mark had everything wired. He could tell when anyone entered the chicken house or opened the stable doors or went near his boat or even left the house. For four months he had had a ham operator's license although he had to borrow Mr. Stone's shortwave set to get it. Sam had no idea how her brother knew all these things, how he could do things like transforming a mess of old wires, rusty razor blades, and discarded radio parts into a warning system that worked. Their father said he was going to be an electronics genius and their mother said he was handy.

"It's Uncle Everett and the rest of them," Mark said.

He and Sam were lying on their backs in the bottom of the empty swimming pool, staring up at the rectangle of bright Montana sky that roofed the clearing. The swimming pool had never had water in it except rain and melting snow. Their father had had it dug when he bought the island and built the house for their mother. Afterward it turned out to be too much trouble to pipe water into the pool, so it lay empty, a neat, Olympic-sized rectangle, hacked out of the rich forest floor.

Today the debris on the bottom was warmed by the September sun, and it was like lying on a mattress. They felt cozy and safe. Unless a person came to the edge and looked in, he would not know they were there.

"I wish my name were something else," Sam said.

Mark looked mildly surprised. "Why?"

"Sam is a foolish name for a fifteen-year-old girl. I wish I were Bonnie May. Or Patricia."

Mark made a nauseated sound. "Or Little Orphan Annie."

"Well, how would you like to have a girl's name?"

Mark ignored the question. "If you had a different name, you'd be somebody else."

"That's ridiculous," Sam said.

Mark picked up the old spy glass that he had found in the town dump and squinted at the tops of the giant evergreens. "The mountain jay is back." He pointed to the swift flash that flared like a blue flame up the side of a yellow pine. "He knows the island is the best place."

Their island was three miles long and a mile and a half across at its widest point. To the west the primitive area stretched off up the Rockies. The town lay east, five minutes from their dock when the outboard was working, or a long walk if you went up to the northeast end of the island, where the river came into the lake, and you could walk across to the mainland in swirling knee-deep water most of the time. South of them the lake narrowed again into the Harshman River.

"It's nice in here today," Mark said, "like bears in a den." He spoke softly so that he would not be heard by the adults, whose voices filtered down through the soft air.

Sam stretched out her legs and regarded her upturned toes. "Sometimes I feel as if I'm in a coffin."

"Coffins have satin and stuff inside," Mark said. "Not that it matters, I guess, if you're dead."

"Where did you ever see a coffin?" Sam asked.

"Oh, last week Pat Allen and I were supposed to carry Miss Barracini's cello to the funeral parlor so she could play at a funeral. Only we got in the wrong room. The dead part."

Sam looked at him with interest. "You didn't tell me."

He shrugged. Sometimes she got the idea that there were a lot of things he didn't tell her. It made her nervous. She wanted to know as much as she could about the world, as fast as possible. "Was anybody in there?"

"Some lady. Well, used to be a lady. From Polson, the tag said."

"How did she look?"

"Sort of like the elk head at Uncle Everett's house. All there, you know, and yet not all there. Like a picture."

They were quiet for a while. They could hear the voices of their parents and Uncle Ev and Aunt Martha, and the clink of glasses and rattle of ice. Sometimes Aunt Martha's voice shrilled above the others, or her laugh shattered like glass, and always there was the creak of her chair as she rocked her great bulk back and forth. It occurred to Sam that Aunt Martha would need a special coffin built for her when she died.

"Do you think they make coffins to fit each person," she said, "or do they come in standard sizes, like shoes and things?"

"You're nutty," Mark said.

"What do you think it's like to be dead?"

Mark shrugged. "I guess your atoms just get arranged in a different way."

"I don't want mine different."

"Who's going to ask you?"

"Mother says you're atom-happy." She put out her hands, pressing them palm down on the solid, sun-warm concrete, feeling the sharpness of pine needles.

Mark turned on his side and examined her with the detached gaze that made her feel like a tadpole in a Mason jar. "You'll be grown-up pretty soon."

"Well, so will you," Sam said. She felt uneasy.

"Not for a while yet. Anyway I don't intend to mix much with people. They're the ones who care how old you are."

"You can't get away from people," Sam said. This was an idea that had come over her lately, causing her some surprise. "That's what Dad tried to do and look at him."

"He didn't try hard enough," Mark said. "He likes to live a little way off and keep popping in on people to see how foolish they are. I think you have to stay really away."

"Don't you like people at all?"

"Sure I do. They're OK. They're fun to watch. I just don't want to get too mixed up with them." He looked at her. "Do you intend to stay here forever?"

"No." Sam wasn't sure what she wanted but she knew it couldn't be just the island. There was a huge world to discover. Going to school had opened up new areas that she had never thought of, even with the books she had read. The island was all the life she had ever known, except for things like shopping trips. "There's so much to see."

"Like what?"

"Oh, like where Keats lived."

"What do you want to see that for?"

"It must be pretty."

"It's pretty here."

"But Keats didn't live here. I just want to see it, that's all."

"What else?" Expertly, Mark caught a dragon fly, examined it, and let it go.

"Oh, the Sphinx and Mt. Fujiyama and the Catacombs. And I want to see if the Tower of Pisa really leans, because I don't believe it."

"Who cares?"

"Me. I want to travel all over. I want to see all kinds of animals. I'd like to buy an Arabian and maybe raise them. And Manx cats. And dogs, of course. I want to raise all kinds of crazy animals and travel around the world with them."

"Maybe Dad will let you have a Shropshire." Mark grinned at her.

7

"Not sheep," Sam said.

"Well, we've got some good Angus," Mark said. "And a couple of Border collies. And banty roosters. And the heifer."

She knew Mark was teasing her now. "You can't even make friends with those border collies," she said. "I'd like to raise Pekingese or Weimaraner or something."

"Never heard of them," Mark said.

"I read more than you do," Sam said. She knew that wasn't true. She just read different kinds of things. "Anyway, I want to *see* everything." She felt cross because she couldn't explain it better. Sometimes the longing for experience, for people and places, was as sharp as salt on her tongue.

"You're nuts." Mark sprang up and teetered on the toes of his gym shoes and caught the end of the diving board. As he pulled his long thin body out of the pool, Aunt Martha gave a little shriek.

"Mark," his mother said, "you shouldn't leap out at people like that."

He stood looking at them, as Sam, wraithlike, rose to join him. Their mother, small and pretty, held out a plate of cookies. Their father, a Coke bottle in his hand, stood apart from the group. His boots were muddy from the meadow where his sheep grazed. Aunt Martha rocked recklessly, and Uncle Everett, round-faced and smiling, pivoted on his chair in order to miss nothing.

"Listen, everybody," Uncle Everett said excitedly. "Listen to old Uncle Ev. We're all going to the carnival tonight. I'm treating. Everybody in his best bib and tucker. We're out on the town tonight."

Sam took her horse out for a ride before dinner. At

the place where the island almost touched the mainland, she crossed over. The river was running withers-high in the middle. Her horse kicked up the water, and Sam wrapped her feet around the saddle horn to protect her boots. Her mother felt bad when she got those boots wet. Her father had paid a lot for them and brought them all the way from New York City the last time he went to a mining engineers' convention. He liked good leather.

As they reached the other side and clambered up the short, steep, root-scarred bank, Sam looked back. The autumn sun lit up the colored world behind her with almost painful vividness. Even the air seemed drenched in color.

She turned from it reluctantly. If she was not to miss the carnival, she must get home. She put her feet down in the stirrups and leaned forward with her arms around her horse's neck. "Autumn is just about too much," she said aloud.

The horse nickered, and tossed his head to the side a few times. On the last try he caught Sam's red hunting cap in his teeth and tossed it to the ground. Sam laughed and slid out of the saddle to get it.

"You want me to get shot at or something?" she said. Hunting seasons opens today, and you know how those guys are."

She remounted and let the horse take his head back across the river and down the faint trail into the cool stillness of the island. The evergreens soared up around her, shutting out the sky.

The horse tensed and sidestepped. Sam listened intently. "You hear a gun or what? I didn't hear anything."

The island was posted, but once in a while her father

gave someone permission to hunt there, and sometimes hunters just came anyway. Poachers made him angry and he had them arrested if he caught up with them. He himself never hunted. It was only Uncle Everett who did.

Every year he spent part of his vacation with them. He and her mother were the only members of their big family who kept track of each other. Sam was always glad to see him because he was jolly and because he always brought presents. For the last three or four years, since the season in their area had begun to open in September, he had taken to hunting on one day of the visit. He would get up at dawn and go out alone with his expensive rifle. So far he hadn't brought back anything except one mangled deer. Her father had been amused at the idea of Everett, railroad man and city man, playing the role of the mighty hunter. 'Uncle Nimrod' he called him. But after the episode of the deer he stopped joking about it.

Mark of course had had a fit. And after she saw that buck, torn by clumsiness, she had agreed with her brother about the hunting. But it was unlikely that Uncle Everett would ever hit anything again, he was such a bad shot.

A small white feather floated down, slantwise, from a jack pine. Sam reached out and caught it. It was soft and tipped with light brown. She smoothed it out gently with her finger and peered up into the tree although she knew she would not see its owner. Somewhere high above her a snowy owl had its nest. She put the feather in her pocket for Mark.

Again she felt the horse stiffen, and at the same time she was aware of a movement like a shadow at her right.

She tightened her legs and spoke soothingly to the horse until he quieted. She stood up in her stirrups to see what had spooked him.

"Ho, boy," she said softly. "Easy, boy."

Then she saw what it was. He was standing behind a chokecherry tree, blending with the gray of the brush behind him. At first she thought it was an enormous wolf but then she saw that it was a huge, long-legged dog with a light-gray, shaggy coat. He had a fine big head, and, it seemed to her, the most intelligent and gentle eyes she had ever seen in an animal.

Cautiously she dismounted and went toward him. The dog watched her, not alarmed but intent. He stood so still that he seemed a part of the forest. Around his neck there was a narrow red collar with a brass nameplate. She tilted her head, trying to read the inscription.

"Here, boy," she said, tentatively holding out her hand.

He made no move, either of advance or retreat. He simply watched her with that detached and faintly interested gaze. Sam was tall for her age but the dog's head was on a level with her chest. When she was close enough, she put out her hand slowly and touched his neck. It did not occur to her to be afraid of him. Murmuring reassuringly, she moved the collar slightly so that she could read part of it. She made out the name "McDermott."

In some distant part of the woods a shot rang out. With a bound the dog was gone. He melted into the woods as if he had never been there. Sam called and whistled. He was gone. She mounted her horse and rode home.

"HE WAS AN IRISH WOLFHOUND," HER FATHER SAID. HE
was kneeling beside his three-foot-high smokehouse.
Uncle Everett perched on a stump, watching him.

"Sure," Uncle Everett said, "like the Russian big
shots used to have in the old days. I seen pictures of
them. Say, I wonder what happened to them dogs. You
suppose Stalin liquidated them?" He slapped his knee,
his round face breaking up into new folds.

"No," her father said, "you're thinking of Russian
wolfhounds—Borzois. Quite different. The Irish resem-
bles the Scottish deerhound except that he is bigger
boned."

Neatly he stacked the cherry logs into the little
camper's stove and tested the pipe that attached the stove
to the smokehouse. From the wicker creel beside him he
took out eight cleaned sockeye salmon and hung them
on the racks inside. With ceremonial intentness he lighted
a fire in the stove.

As the kindling caught and crackled he rose. He was a tall angular man with brown hair already receding along his bony temples. The long-jawed sensitive face, the half-melancholy, half-derisive gray eyes framed in dark-rimmed glasses, the old tweed jacket with leather-patched sleeves, the khaki wash pants several inches too short, all suggested a professor rather than a rancher and miner.

"The apple wood is better," he said, "but I'm saving that for the trout."

"It beats me," Everett said, "why a man would go to all that trouble. Me, I'll take my fish and meat straight, thank you. No blacking them all up with smoke for me." He tossed away the burned-down cigar and leaned forward.

For a second Sam had a vision of Uncle Everett stretched out on the rack of some larger smokehouse.

"It's all a matter of taste, Ev," her father said. He reached out his foot and ground the glowing cigar butt into the ground.

"Oh-oh. Sorry, Albert," Uncle Everett said. "Forgot about Smoky Bear."

"But Daddy, what would he be doing on this island? The dog, I mean," Sam said.

"I met a man named McDermott at Pete's place," her father said. "I told him he could hunt here. He's after timber wolves."

"Timber wolves!" Everett looked over his shoulder. "You're kidding, Al."

"We have a few," Albert said. "They come across from the primitive area." He opened the stove lid and poked gently at the logs. "Anyway this McDermott said he raised Irish wolfhounds."

"You mean he has a kennel?" Sam said.

Her father looked at her with dry amusement. "I don't suppose he keeps them in the bathroom."

Everett hooted with laughter. He rocked until he nearly fell off the stump. "Keeps them in the bathroom," he gasped. "Oh, that's a dandy. Albert, you're a card."

Sam liked her uncle but there were times, especially this year, when she felt that he was not very bright. She had spoken to Mark about it but he only said that he had never considered Uncle Everett bright. "I'm surprised he knows which end of his rifle scope to look through," he had said. "Someday he'll wind up on somebody's trophy wall."

Sam looked away from her uncle, embarrassed by his giggling. "Well," she said, "I'd sure like to have one of those dogs." She polished the toes of her boots with a Kleenex, trying to seem casual.

"An Irish?" her father said. "You're crazy. He'd eat us out of house and home."

"I'd work for his food," she said quickly. "Honest."

Uncle Everett swayed in another spasm of mirth. "I can see you now, Sammy, running around with a big, skinny, narrow-headed critter trotting after you, begging for a bone." He took off his rimless glasses and mopped his eyes.

"He isn't skinny and narrow-headed," Sam said. "He's beautiful."

"You're thinking of Borzois, Everett," Albert said patiently. "No, Sam, it's out of the question. Even a puppy would cost four or five hundred dollars." He started up the path, with his long and slightly lopsided gait. "Better wash up for dinner if you're going to the carnival with us."

Uncle Everett sobered. "Don't you feel bad, honey," he said. "Maybe if you was to go to the pound, you could find you a nice little dog."

"I don't want a nice little dog," she said. "I want one of those." She sighed. "I don't mean to sound like a brat. It's just that sometimes you just want something."

"I know how that is," he said He stared past her for a moment. Then he got up, patting his stomach in Santa Claus fashion. "Yep, I know how that is, all righty."

Sam looked at him with interest. It had never occurred to her that a grown man might want something that he could not go right out and get. As they started toward the house she had to look down at him because already she was four inches taller than he was. It struck her that Uncle Everett was getting old. He had the look of an apple that has begun to wither. In an effort to be nice to him she asked him questions about his Butte-to-Missoula run, although she had been hearing about it all her life.

"You must get awful sick of it," she said. "Butte to Missoula, Missoula to Butte, day after day. The train must seem more like home than your own house."

He gave a funny little inward chuckle. "You just don't know how sick of it a man can get. No, sir, you just don't know."

"I bet Aunt Martha gets pretty lonesome, too, you riding that old train all the time, and no kids and all." For a moment Sam imagined the loneliness of Martha's life and she made a quick resolution to be nicer to her.

"I guess she's used to it," Uncle Everett said.

"I suppose so."

Later as she and Mark cleaned up for dinner, she said, "He looked so kind of funny and pathetic."

"Oh, don't bother about them," Mark said, giving the pronoun the slight emphasis that he used to indicate adults. "Wait till you see my neat new boat."

"What is it?" She wanted to tell him about the dog, but she couldn't seem to speak of it yet.

"It's part of a cement mixer. Not the part that swirls around but the big metal pan they stir it in after it's swirled. I'm putting in a wooden floor. It's going to be great."

Their mother's voice called them from downstairs.

"I don't know why she doesn't use that buzzer system I fixed," he said. "Saves all that yelling."

When they were finishing their dessert Mark said to his mother, "If we only had a maid, I could fix up one of those deals where you step on a button under the table and the maid comes tearing in from the kitchen."

Babe laughed. "I see myself with a maid."

"Gracious, you don't need one," Aunt Martha said. "Look, Ev, honey, ain't that handy the way that counter just separates the dining room and the kitchen? And all those lovely built-ins. It's just like *Better Homes and Gardens*."

"I had to promise Babe a dream house so she'd marry me," Albert said. He pushed back his chair and hung one leg over the arm.

Babe looked at him with tolerant disapproval. She was eight years younger than he was, and sometimes he treated her like one of his children.

"I remember your wedding like it was yesterday." Martha's shrill voice softened in sentimental reverie. "Children, you should have seen that wedding."

"Good thing they didn't," Albert said. "They'd have been hard to explain."

Sam signaled discreetly to her mother to be excused, but her mother frowned. Mark and Sam exchanged despairing glances.

"It took me four years to get her to marry me, Martha, don't forget that."

"Well, she was too young," Everett said. "You take a kid that age, she don't know her own mind."

Sam tried to imagine her mother, seventeen years old, two years older than she was now, being courted.

"Anyway," Martha said, not to be done out of her memory, "Your father told her, 'I got this island I found on a fishing trip'—that's how he found this island, on a fishing trip—'and I'm going to build you a house on it,' he told her."

"And I did, and here we are," said Albert. He was getting tired of the story.

Mark's fingers clenched the edge of the table in an involuntary impulse of escape, but no one made a move to rise.

Then Babe pushed back her chair and Mark shot out of his. "If we're going to the carnival," she said, "we'd better get ready."

"Can I wear the sweater Uncle Ev gave me?" Sam asked.

"Yes," her mother said, "if you'll be careful of it."

"I really love it," Sam said to her uncle. "The kids at school will really envy me."

"And isn't that a noble goal," Albert said. "That's one example of why I didn't let my kids go to school until last January."

"You must be an awful smart man, Albert, teaching them yourself all these years," Martha said.

"It doesn't take a genius to keep abreast of the public

school system," Albert said. "Or slightly ahead of."

"They're too young for the grades they're in," Babe said. "Sam shouldn't be a junior, she's not old enough. And Mark has no business being a sophomore."

"Which proves my point." Albert pushed back his chair.

Babe shook her head, but said no more.

"I got a real deal on those sweaters," Everett said. "I know this salesman, he rides my run pretty regular. Sweaters, jackets, stuff like that. He's got some kind of a little system worked out. I don't know just what it is, but some way he ends up with a parcel of merchandise left over every month. So now and then he lets me have a couple of things at cost."

Albert raised his eyebrows. "Hot sweaters?"

"It sounds dishonest," Babe said.

"You got to admire a guy that can figure out a little something and make a go of it. It's American initiative, that's what it is." Uncle Everett lighted a cigar.

"If it's dishonest, its dishonest," Babe said.

"Are you prepared to give back the sweater?" Albert asked her.

"That isn't the point . . ."

"It's exactly the point. If you're going to be righteous, you have to go all the way."

"Mom, I don't have to give back the sweater, do I?" Sam said.

"Oh—" Defeated, Babe turned away and went into the kitchen.

"Well, Albert's a bug on honesty and all that," Everett said. "Like selling that uranium mine just when he was hitting it big. Not only selling it, but giving most of it to his partner's wife."

"Widow," Albert said sharply. "Widow and five children, Everett."

"All right," Everett said. "It done you credit, I'll admit that, Al, but you didn't need to give away your shirt. You had your own family to think of."

Sam hoped her father wouldn't answer, but she knew he would. He always had to explain all over again about selling the mine.

"My family isn't exactly starving," Albert said. His mouth was tight. "I had an obligation to the Gateses. Joe was my partner. He was shot down in cold blood by a claim jumper, you know that."

"They were shooting each other all over the place during that uranium boom."

"Half of what I owned belonged to his family."

"But you gave 'em most of it. And why sell at all? That's what always got me. You could have made a million."

"I'm happy here, raising good sheep."

Babe came in and put her hand on her brother's shoulder. "Come on," she said, "let's all cheer up now and have a nice time at the carnival."

Everett brightened. "Is everybody ready? Sam, get your sweater on. Where's Mark?"

"He went upstairs," Sam said. She rummaged around in the hall closet for her new sweater. It was still in its box. She took it out and held it against her cheek.

In the dining room she saw Uncle Everett helping Aunt Martha to her feet. There was a moment of braced muscles and drawn breath, and she was up. She swayed a little and grabbed the chair.

"Oh, my," she said. She waddled across the room like an elderly duck, and clutched the copper hood of the fireplace in the corner. "Oh, dear."

Everett looked at her suspiciously. "Now what?"

"I feel a migraine coming on." She put her hand to her head as if it were fragile and might come off. "I declare, I don't believe I'll be able to go."

Everett groaned. "I knew it. Every time."

"No, no," Martha said, "you all just run along. I'll just lie on the couch . . ."

"There's no TV, you know," Everett said, with a touch of malice. "My wife is on TV like some folks are on heroin."

"I can't help it, can I," Martha said, "if I get one of those miserable headaches? Perhaps the dinner was too rich. Not that it wasn't lovely, Babe, I don't mean that. It's just my foolish, old head."

"You go lie down, Martha," Babe said. "I'll get you a cold cloth." To Albert she said, "I'll stay home with her."

"Oh, I don't want to spoil your evening, Babe," Martha said hopefully. "Although it is a little bit scary out here in the woods alone . . ."

"For the love of Pete," Everett protested. "Babe's been looking forward to the carnival."

"No," Babe said firmly. "I don't really care. You and Albert take the children. Warm coats, everybody. The nights are getting cold."

Albert gave Babe a raised-eyebrows look of resignation and said, "All right, let's go." He went into the hall and called, "Mark, hurry up."

Mark flew down the stairs, and there was a last minute confusion that seemed to fill up the wide hall. Babe was buttoning down the hood of Sam's parka. From the living room couch Martha waved a languid good-by.

Everett reached up and touched the gilded eagle that formed the design at the top of the hall mirror. "I'd like to shoot me one of them."

"Why do you want to shoot everything?" Sam asked.

"I guess that's just the spirit of the hunter, like they say. You ladies are different. Right, Albert?"

"I have no idea," Albert said. "I'm not a hunter."

As soon as they left the house and moved beyond the lemon disc of light that encircled the front steps, the black night engulfed them They went in silent single file along the path through the woods. Albert led the way and Everett brought up the rear. The thin ray of Albert's flashlight made a bobbing pattern on the ground.

It was almost half a mile to the boat landing. Everett began to puff in his effort to keep up. In his hurry he stubbed his toe.

Albert stopped and glanced back as he heard the crashing sound that Everett made. "You still on your feet, Ev?"

"Oh, sure." Everett tried to sound hearty but his voice shook in spite of him. "I knew Martha wouldn't come," he said. "She don't like them sideshows on account of the fat lady." He hurried to catch up with them as if nothing had happened.

Sam looked at him, shocked at the malice in his tone when he spoke of Aunt Martha. It was not kind to make fun of her weight. She heard him mutter annoyance as a branch scraped his face. He kept looking nervously from side to side. It occurred to her that the woods really frightened him.

"You ought to carry a gun, Albert," he said, "roaming around these woods at night like this."

Albert held up the light so he could see Everett's

face. "You feeling jumpy, Ev?"

"Of course not," Everett said crossly. "Just thinking of you and the kids. These woods must be full of wolves and things."

"They won't bother us unless they're hungry," Mark said. "Or unless it's rutting deer in the spring."

There was a great whoosh of sound and something smacked Everett on the shoulder. There was a churning of air and a hoarse cry. He lurched forward in terror and fell headlong.

He was trembling all over and almost in tears when Sam and Albert helped him up. "Mountain lion . . . or wolf . . . or something . . . jumped me." He touched his shoulder fearfully, feeling for blood.

"It was just a snowy owl, Uncle Ev," Sam said.

"Owl!" He almost sobbed. "Owl nothing. It was an animal. It jumped me, I tell you. And you know I got this heart condition."

"Look." Sam put two snowy brown-tipped feathers in his shaking hand. "She was more scared than you."

He stared unbelievingly at the soft feathers.

"She ran into you. They don't see well." Albert brushed off Everett's jacket.

"Everbody knows owls can see at night," Everett snapped.

Albert was growing impatient. "We're right at the end of the path now." He flashed the light to show Everett the clearing.

The river was black velvet. Overhead the stars glittered, almost close enough to touch. The forest behind them looked closed now, impenetrable as a fortress.

There was a clank of sound, instantly lost in the night, as Albert unlocked the boathouse. He and Mark eased the boat into the water. The stern lifted and dipped and rode easy, white on black.

Albert hung one leg over the bow and looked back. "All aboard."

The children waited politely while Uncle Everett hoisted his short legs over the gunwales. Then they clambered in and sat together on the seat near the stern. Uncle Everett sat in front of them, his back to them, stiff and silent. Albert bent over the motor and yanked the cord. His temples gleamed whitely. The motor sputtered and died. He tried again and it caught.

The putt-putt of the outboard was the only sound in the night as the bow of the boat cut a moving V in the dark water. In about five minutes the shadowy outline of the dock came into view. Albert shut off the engine and Mark moved into the bow to seize the piling and smooth the boat in. He scrambled up onto the dock and attached the mooring chain. They all sat in the boat looking up at his crouched figure above them and for a moment no one made a move to get out. The boat rocked gently on its own wash, and the slap of the water against the boat and the dock held more stillness than sound.

"All out," Albert said. "Off to Babylon."

They drove in the pickup to the vacant lot across the street from the carnival. Garish lights strung on wire enclosed the area of the show, turning the air purple and red and orange. The colors were repeated and varied over and over in the canopies and booths and the clothes of the swarming crowd.

Uncle Everett was swelling up with good cheer. He took out his big gold watch and looked at it, his eyes glazed with joy. "Come on, everybody," he cried. And he herded them across the street.

As they came close, a medley of sounds hit out at them, the loud talk and laughter blunted into a single roar punctuated by the fast chatter of the barkers. The public address system blared rock and roll. The carousel music tinkled, and a Viennese waltz accompanied the loop-the-loop, dipping and soaring like a brash young bird.

Mark broke away from them and prowled the edges of the crowd, watching. Sam saw her father shudder and pull back as the crowd jostled him. Uncle Everett breathed deep and happy lungfuls of the smoky air.

"Live it up," he said to no one in particular. "Old Uncle Ev is paying for everything."

"Ev," Albert said, "why don't you and the kids go on and enjoy yourselves. I'll meet you later." He moved aside in distaste as a couple of teen-age girls careened against him.

Everett grabbed him by the arm. "Nothing doing, Al. You gotta come with us. Let yourself go, man. Enjoy yourself."

Albert gave up, and the three of them were caught up in the crowd, swept along like sticks in a whirlpool. At the vortex stood the Ferris wheel. The crowd was converging on it, pointing up and laughing. Uncle Everett tugged at Albert's arm, and in a moment they were standing at the base of the wheel.

Something was wrong. The wheel had stopped turning. It gave Sam a feeling of shock to look up at it. It hung motionless, each light and each part now separate fragments. Some boys climbed down and jumped to the ground but at the top a boy and a girl sat, clinging to the rail. The crowd shouted ribald advice to the boy. He grinned foolishly and gave a fluttery little wave. The motion rocked the seat, and the girl cried out. Uncle Everett was shaking all over with laughter.

Sam was frightened. She looked at her father. He pushed his way to the operator of the wheel, who was struggling to get it going. The operator was a thin, uncertain-looking man, and the trouble he was having with the wheel made him so nervous that he fumbled ineffectually with the machinery. The crowd shouted at him in good-natured derision.

"How does it work?" Albert yelled in his ear.

The operator looked at him doubtfully.

Someone on the ground gave the bottom of the wheel a shove. It tilted backward a little and the girl screamed.

Albert pushed the operator aside and peered at the gears and levers. The operator shrugged and made a gesture to the crowd, as if to say it was not his fault if fools interfered.

Sam held her breath and watched as her father worked on the gear that seemed to be stuck. She suddenly saw him alone against the world, and it frightened her. The crowd didn't want him to fix the machinery. They were enjoying the diversion of the stranded boy and girl. Some of the younger men started pushing toward Albert as if to prevent him from getting the wheel fixed. Then with a slow clanking and grinding, the wheel began to turn. Albert stood up, his hair falling forward over his forehead, frowning upward to make sure the wheel was working. In that moment, in his concentration and his obliviousness to the crowd, he seemed heroic to Sam.

Now that the crisis was over, people began to drift

away. The boy and girl in their slow descent looked at each other at last. The boy put his arm around the girl, and a few people cheered. She smiled and fluffed out her hair. They stepped out stiffly as if they had been immobilized for hours. The boy struck a cocky pose and the girl looked up at him adoringly.

"I'll meet you in the pickup at ten," Albert said to Everett, and disappeared. No one, thought Sam, even thanked him.

Sam stayed with Uncle Everett, catching the mood of his gaiety. They rode the merry-go-round, Sam on a purple camel and Uncle Ev on a pink pony with rhinestone eyes. She clutched his arm in delightful terror as the whip snapped them around. After the loop-the-loop they paused for greasy foot-long hot dogs smeared with bright yellow mustard. They rocked with laughter at the sight of themselves in the hall of mirrors. In front of one mirror Sam saw Uncle Ev, tremendously elongated, grinning at her in such a droop-eyed and sinister fashion that she had to look at the real Uncle Ev to reassure herself.

It was true all right that Uncle Ev knew how to enjoy life. Maybe that was one of the keys to happiness. Sam had become quite concerned lately with what she thought of, in capital letters, as KEYS TO HAPPINESS. In her Book of Thoughts, where she kept quotations that seemed at the time important, she had recently included the saying, "We only go this way once," although the grammar bothered her.

Once, while they were gulping hot coffee, she saw Mark threading his way like a thin ghost through the edges of the crowd. She tried to signal to him, but he either did not see her or chose to ignore her.

With sticky streaks of candied apple on her chin she

clung to Uncle Everett through the insane movements of the octopus. Lurching a little and feeling pleasantly sick she let herself be guided through the tents that housed the tatooed man, the bearded lady, and the the grotesquely simpering dwarfs. At the throne of the fat lady, however, she turned away. The lady herself had disappeared and a barker was hoarsely urging them to pay their money and come inside. If Uncle Everett had not said that about Aunt Martha, when they were in the forest, Sam might not have minded seeing the fat lady, but he had said it and she could not bring herself to go in and stare. She excused herself and left Uncle Everett, who was eagerly pushing his way inside.

In a few minutes, as she was wandering aimlessly, she saw Mark beckoning. She followed him into the mysterious unlighted area behind the exhibits. He pointed to a torn place in the canvas of one of the tents, held up a warning finger to his lips, and then squirmed through it and out of sight. She managed to force herself through the gap and found him crouching in darkness behind a raised platform. She could see the lighted surface of the stage and the backs of the performers from the knees up.

A scratchy recording of *Scheherezade* played somewhere out of sight. On stage a man in a swirling black cape and a tall black hat was moving rapidly around the small platform swooping and darting like a big bat. His assistant, in baggy, blue satin pants, a tight jacket covered with glitter and a red turban, stood beside a big barrel that had been daubed with silver paint and drilled with a series of holes.

The magician swept his arm in a dramatic gesture, and a girl pirouetted onto the stage. She was about twelve years old. She was wearing a ballerina costume with pink frilled tights, a tight bodice and a stand-out skirt made of orange gauze. The crowd stamped and whistled as she whirled around the stage. She paused beside the barrel. Sam could see the tops of her red net stockings and the stiff costume that stuck out in back.

In a ringing voice the magician announced that he would now assist the young princess into the barrel which was, as all could see, quite empty. (Here he motioned imperiously to his assistant, who tipped the barrel forward.). And he would cause the young princess to disappear out of this same barrel which, as they had just seen for themselves, was quite, entirely, completely empty. With a flourish he produced a number of brightly painted sharp-pointed sticks. To prove to the audience that the princess had indeed disappeared, he would hurl the arrows through the holes in the barrel. He pointed out the holes, and the crowd whistled.

Sam shivered and looked at Mark. He made a face to show he didn't believe a word of it.

The music stopped abruptly. "And now, ladies and gentlemen," the magician said in a solemn voice, "we will attempt this feat, unmatched in human history." He waved his hands over the barrel and then helped the girl into it. She disappeared inside, and he made a few more gestures, muttering some kind of incantation.

"The princess has now disappeared," he said. "Were she still within the barrel, she would now suffer a hideous death!" On the word "death" he brought his arm up and down with great force, plunging one of the sharpened sticks through a hole near the top. Then in quick succession he hurled the other sticks through the remaining holes until the barrel was pierced all over.

He bowed elaborately to the applause. "And now by a process mysterious and magic, we will return the little lady to the barrel." Again he made sweeping gestures with his hands over the barrel, and spoke unintelligible words. "Presto! She is here. And those of you who wish to witness this miracle for yourself may come up on the stage and see her . . ." He paused and there was a sound of chairs scraping and people moving. ". . . for the insignificant sum of ten cents, just one thin dime."

Mark poked Sam and held his nose to show his opinion of the act. Then he writhed through the hole in the tent and disappeared. Sam felt in her pocket for a dime. When the magician was at the front of the stage, she scrambled up onto the platform and joined the four people who had come forward. With an effort not to touch him, she dropped her dime into the magician's hand. She looked inside the barrel. The little princess was contorted into a grotesque parody of her dancing self. The wickedly sharp points of the sticks had missed her by fractions of an inch, and they formed a trap that held her motionless. There were three bright drops of blood just above her eye where one point had grazed her.

Sam stared at her in horror until at last the child looked up. Her head was held at an unnatural angle. She looked up at Sam with terrified and unseeing eyes. And soundlessly, she began to cry. The tears smudged her makeup. Sam felt sick but she couldn't look away.

The magician began to remove the sticks, keeping up his patter to the disappearing audience. As each sharp point was jerked past the child's body, she shuddered. The magician noticed Sam. "Come, come, young lady," he said playfully, "we can't have you holding up the procession here." He took her elbow and steered her toward the rickety steps that led down into the gray abyss of the audience.

Sam stepped into the sawdust at the bottom of the steps. She looked up at him. In his long cape he looked immensely tall and his teeth gleamed. The people were almost gone. The magician raised his voice. "Tell your friends about us. Tell them about the little princess who disappears." He swooped down and helped the girl out of the barrel. She whirled around the stage like a pink and orange dragonfly. The few people still in the tent applauded tepidly. She danced offstage and the magician bowed and the curtain creaked and whined on its pulleys, narrowing the visible area of the stage down and down until there was nothing.

A man and his wife and daughter pushed by Sam. "Pretty clever the way he does that," he said.

"It's all fake." The wife sounded bored. "Those sticks are probably rubber."

"I don't know," he said. "They looked real to me."

The young girl said, "Oh, Daddy, don't be naive. It isn't real."

Sam was left alone in the tent. She went to the back and sat down gingerly on one of the rickety folding chairs. It was dark and there was a smell of sawdust and sweat. In a minute the curtain was jerked back and a work light went on, a single bulb that cast a sharp white circle in the center of the platform. The assistant shuffled out, wearing a dirty white coverall. His greasy blond hair fell over his forehead. He leaned against the barrel and lighted a cigarette. He was listening with a fixed moronic smile to the wrangling voices offstage.

"If you don't break down and buy a needle," a shrill female voice said, "one of these nights you won't have no offstage music."

"Where's that kid?" It was the magician's voice, with the smoothness gone out of it. "Listen, kid, if I catch you bawling onstage again, I'll really give you something to bawl about, you understand me?"

"Was she bawling?" The woman laughed. "How about that."

"You hear me, kid?" There was the sound of a slap and a muffled sob.

The assistant teetered up and down in silent mirth.

"You, Murdock," the magician yelled. "Strike those props. We got to get out of here by midnight."

"Yuh." Taking his time, the assistant rolled the barrel offstage. The work light went out.

Sam sat still in the dark. She wished she were back in the familiar rectangle of the swimming pool, watching the sky through the trees.

She got up and fumbled for the opening flap in the tent. Uncle Ev would be wondering where she was. Uncle Ev didn't seem to get all shook about things. Except in the woods sometimes. She wished she were as sure of things as Uncle Ev seemed to be. She thought of how often he took out that big gold watch and held it in his hand. "Never a minute off," he always said. Never slow, never fast.

Outside, she blinked in the glare of the lights. She thought she would like to find Uncle Everett and ask him if she could hold his watch for a minute.

She saw him at the Midway. He was aiming a rifle at a row of jerking ducks. He would almost certainly miss. He was such a terrible shot. "Uncle Ev," she called. And she went toward him with tears blinding her eyes.

SAM AND ALBERT FACED EACH OTHER ACROSS THE BLUE formica table in Babe's immaculate kitchen. The cup of coffee in Albert's hand sent up a thin feather of steam. Sam was spreading peanut butter on a piece of bread.

"But I didn't *do* anything," she said. "I didn't even say anything."

"It wouldn't have done any good," Albert said.

"Well, I would have felt better."

He turned the cup of coffee slowly in his hands. "That's it, you see. Sometimes one makes a protest just because he feels he has to, but if he looks at what he's really doing, he may find that he's just trying to give himself an out."

"What do you mean?"

"If something is wrong and it's beyond our power to change it, and we feel guilty anyway, then we may kick up a little fuss just to make ourselves feel better. It may simply cause more trouble."

"You mean if I had kicked up a stink, I might have got that little princess girl into worse trouble?"

"Yes, but don't say 'stink.' Your mother doesn't like it."

"But there must be something somebody could do." She bit into her sandwich. "Why are people so mean to each other?"

Sam was silent for a while, eating her sandwich and thinking. "Sometimes I wish we lived in town," she said.

He looked shocked. "Leave the island?"

"Not really leave it altogether. But I get to wishing we had television, and a back yard barbecue, and neighbors."

"The forest is your picnic area," he said. "The animals are your neighbors, and they're a lot safer than people."

Sam sighed. "I guess so."

"Let's clear this stuff away." He got up and put the milk into the refrigerator.

"Thanks anyway for having a serious talk with me," Sam said.

He smiled. "Courtesy of the house."

Babe appeared in the doorway, sleepy, with her hair hanging loosely over her shoulders. "Will you wild Indians go to bed?"

"We had to discuss things," Sam said.

Babe got the dishcloth and wiped up a few crumbs from the table top.

"I suppose Ev is still going hunting in the morning," Albert said.

"He plans to."

"I hope he won't see any game."

"How was the carnival?"

"Horrible," Albert said.

Babe yawned. "Carnivals are trashy."

Albert laughed. "Sam, I hope you'll turn out like your mother. She doesn't torment herself with doubts. She just *knows*."

"It doesn't take all that to know about carnivals," Babe said. "Sam, what are you doing?"

"I just want to get some lettuce for Miss Alice."

"No wonder I can't get ahead," Albert said. "I feed too many animals."

"A guinea pig doesn't eat much," Sam said. She went out into the back hall and gave the lettuce to her guinea pig, who lived in a cardboard box. When she came back, she said, "I suppose you did mean no, about the Irish wolfhound?"

"I did mean no," Albert said.

"That's what I thought," Sam said. "Well, good night." She ran up the stairs.

C745787

SAM WOKE UP SHIVERING. A STORM HAD COME DURING the night. There were streaks of cold rain on her casement windows and the early morning light made a thin shifting diagram on her bedroom floor. She pulled the blankets up around her neck.

She searched her memory for the tag end of a dream that she had had. It was about a dog, an Irish wolfhound that had moved like a shadow through the trees, always just out of reach.

She lay still, thinking about the dog. Someday she would make some money and buy one just like him. But someday was not now, and it was now that she wanted him. She turned over, hunching the blankets around her shoulder. For a second she felt angry with her father for refusing to get her an Irish. But in the midst of the thought she remembered that there were things he wanted for himself that he did not buy. Some more Shropshires, for instance.

Uncle Ev was the only one who understood how she felt about the dog, though. He had been nice about it. She felt a warm glow of affection for Uncle Ev. And a moment later she heard him go softly down the stairs. She sat up, surprised. She would not have expected him to go hunting in this cold, drizzling weather. He hated to be uncomfortable. She listened intently. Perhaps he had just gone downstairs for a snack. She considered joining him. It would be warmer in the kitchen. She got up and padded across the cold floor to the closet and put on her warm bathrobe and slippers.

As she went past Mark's room, she heard the faint whirr of his warning system. Uncle Everett must have left the house already. She went into Mark's room and looked out the window. She could see Uncle Everett standing near her mother's herb garden. He was standing quite still as if he was listening. The tan material of his quilted jacket made a pale blob in the half-light. There was a canteen slung over his shoulder. He was holding his hunting cap in one hand, and as Sam watched, he thrust his rifle between his knees to support it while he put on his cap. She held her breath until he had the gun in his hand again. It was not that he was reckless. In fact, he handled the gun with a gingerly caution. It was his lack of assurance that was dangerous.

He continued to stand there a moment longer. He looked somehow out of place, almost forlorn. Sam wondered if he would mind if she went along with him. Perhaps the man with the Irish wolfhound would be out hunting again and she would see the dog.

As she passed Mark's bed he sat bolt upright, his eyes wide and alarmed. "What is it?" he said.

"Shh. It's only me."

"OK." He was asleep again in a second.

The buzzer stopped as Uncle Everett moved beyond its range. She went back to her room and pulled on corduroy frontier pants, wool socks, and a flannel shirt. It took a few minutes to find her winter jacket. Carrying her moccasins, she went quietly downstairs. It would not do to awaken her mother, who disapproved of early morning prowling, especially in hunting season.

Uncle Everett had forgotten to turn off the kitchen light, and she was tempted by the snug warmth of the room. After all she did not have to go outside. She could make hot cocoa and turn on the electric panel heater and read. She stood in the kitchen, undecided. A branch of a maple tree outside the window slashed at the glass with a wet sound. Its few remaining leaves had changed overnight from crisp scarlet to sodden brown.

Then she heard her mother stirring, and quickly she unlatched the back door and went out into the gray, dripping world. If she was going to catch up with Uncle Everett, she would have to hurry. She went to the herb garden and found his footsteps heading down the path to the north end of the island. She knew he must have the meadow in mind, for deer. Just so he didn't go off half-cocked and take a potshot at any of her father's sheep. There were half a dozen Shropshires in that meadow.

She walked fast to keep warm. Soon she was gaining on Uncle Everett. The heel marks of his boots, ground into the leaves and pine needles, were no longer nearly obliterated by water. Once she thought she heard the crackling of twigs ahead of her. She slowed down. No need to make Uncle Ev mad, and no need to get shot at either. He might panic and think she was an animal.

She thought about his fear the night before in the woods. It was hard for her to imagine anyone being afraid in the forests unless he actually came face to face with a grizzly or a hungry mountain lion or wolf.

After about fifteen minutes she came to the edge of the meadow. Daylight was making more progress here. At the north end of the field, blurred by the fine rain, the white shapes of the sheep moved lazily. Uncle Everett was nowhere in sight. He was probably holed up somewhere waiting for deer to come into the open field. She sat down on a stump and took off her moccasins, pouring out the water. Her socks were soggy and her corduroy pants were like a wet sponge. Shivering she wrapped her arms around herself, wondering why she had been crazy enough to come out.

Soundlessly, two deer came into the meadow from the west. They bounded so lightly through the slanting rain that they seemed to float. Caught by their grace, Sam watched. She clasped her hands tightly together, praying that Uncle Everett would miss. The image of those beautiful proudly-held antlers fixed to the wall of Uncle Ev's cluttered little den was unbearable.

First the doe and then the buck bent their heads and drank from the narrow creek that cut across the pasture. She waited tensely for the crack of the rifle. Uncle Everett must be taking his time about sighting. With that expensive scope of his, he could hardly miss. The moments passed. The buck tossed his head and bounded easily toward the forest. The doe hesitated a moment and then followed. They were gone.

Puzzled, Sam got up. Perhaps Uncle Everett had circled around and gone home, sick of the weather. A hot shower and breakfast would be good. She turned to go back but curiosity and concern overcame her. Uncle Ev might be in trouble. She left the path and began to make her way with difficulty through the wet scrub that bordered the meadow. She tried to be quiet, but now and then a branch broke with what seemed like a deafening crack in that silent place.

She stopped to catch her breath and to watch a jack rabbit leap for cover. Then she moved on again. It was very still except for the slow drip of water from the trees. The thin, metallic yelp of the border collie who watched the sheep came to her from the far end of the meadow. She parted the branches and peered in that direction, wondering if it were Uncle Everett who had alarmed him.

She decided to turn back. It was clear that Uncle Everett was not hunting in this area. She was on a soggy wild-goose chase. She angled back toward the woods, searching for a little trail that she and Mark had come upon during the summer. It was a short cut to the house.

When she found it, she started to turn left but first, from the habit of keeping alert in the forest, she looked to the right. She stopped. There was a sound. It was so faint that she could not identify it. She bent her head and listened intently. A chipmunk shot past her and up the trunk of a tamarack, scolding all the way.

"Shh!" Sam said.

There was metal in the sound. She wondered if an animal had come upon an old tin pail or can and was banging it on the ground. The sensible thing was to go on home. Prying into the activities of the animals was asking for trouble. But there was a rhythm about the sound, a regularity, that was strange. Perhaps if she walked a little way, she could see without getting too close. She remembered that the path, an old game trail, looped around and ended farther down the meadow.

She moved carefully, bending down to escape over-hanging branches. The sound stopped. She waited. Perhaps the animal had caught her scent. But then it began again, louder and faster. She glanced around from time to time. The sinister gray form of the wolf flashed through her mind; and the thought that now and then one came upon a grizzly, wandering down from the mountains. "The careful person survives," her father had always told them, "not the fearful or the careless one."

She stopped as she heard the metallic sound close by. Kneeling in the bushes she pushed apart the branches in front of her face. She was closer to the meadow than she had realized. Beyond the trees she could see the stiff hummocks of coarse grass and the dip of the coulee.

On the far side of the coulee was Uncle Everett. His back was toward her, and he was bending over, banging his canteen against a rock. He kept hitting it harder and harder, as if he were getting madder and madder.

Relieved to discover that it was only Uncle Ev, Sam straightened up and started to go to him. But she stopped again, puzzled by his odd behavior. He lifted up the canteen and slammed it to the ground and jumped on it.

Sam was suddenly uncomfortably aware that she was spying on him. She stepped forward and gave her coyote bark. Before she could go any further, he grabbed his rifle and fired. The bullet zinged past her and buried itself in a tree. She dropped to the ground. He was waving the gun wildly, not seeing her. He fired again, and the bullet hit the ground, sending up a little shower of dirt. The report of the gun rolled like thunder.

"Uncle Ev! It's me."

He shaded his eyes with his hand. "Where?" His voice sounded cracked and strange. "Who is it?"

"Here. It's me. Sam." Her knees were shaking. She was not sure that Uncle Everett had not gone quite crazy. "I'm coming out now, OK?"

Slowly he lowered the gun. "OK."

She came out of the brush and they stared at each other as if they were strangers.

"What you doing here?" he said, finally.

She had never seen him look so odd. His hunting cap had fallen off and his hair, wet with sweat, was plastered against his head in flat strands. He reminded her of a fox she had cornered once, eyes bright and hard and depthless. She was afraid of him.

"Where did you come from?" he demanded. "What were you chasing after me for?"

"I was just out," Sam said. "I heard a funny noise." She looked at the battered canteen.

He too looked at the canteen and back at her. "How long you been here?"

"Just a few minutes."

There was a silence, and Sam had the feeling that he was wondering what to do with her. "See any game?"

He looked at the gun as if it surprised him to find it there. "No. No game. Not a thing."

"I saw a couple of deer," she said

"Deer? Is that so?" He looked as if he had just recognized her. "I guess you wonder what I'm up to."

"Yes," Sam said. "I did sort of wonder." She had a feeling that it would be wiser to pretend that she had not noticed anything unusual, but she didn't know how to avoid a direct question.

Then all at once he became his old self. "It was just

that you took me kind of sudden, coming up on me like that. It's a wonder I didn't shoot at you."

"You did," she said, "but you missed."

"Sam," he said, shocked. "Never come up quick on anybody like that. You might get hurt. Always sing out first."

"I did sing out," she said "Is anything wrong, Uncle Ev?"

He hesitated. Then he said, "I can't get the canteen open." He looked as if he wanted to cry.

"The top is off."

"I mean *open*. I got to get some stuff out of it."

Sam thought he was having what Aunt Martha would call a little early morning snort of whiskey, and that he was reluctant to say so. "Can't you just tip it up and pour it out?"

With great irritation he said, "It doesn't pour."

Sam was mystified. What would you have in a canteen that didn't pour? "Is it frozen or something?"

"Not hardly."

She knew she was exasperating him. "What is in there, Uncle Ev, if you don't mind my asking?"

"Money," he said. He shook the canteen. "Money, money, money. And how do I walk into a bank and say, 'Please change this canteen into travelers' checks?'"

"Money?" It made no sense at all.

"Well, I had to put it somewhere. Martha goes through my pockets with a fine-tooth comb. And she pounces on the bank statement like a. . . " He broke off.

"I can probably get the top off the canteen if you don't mind my wrecking it," Sam said. She fished in her pockets for her Scout knife and opened the can opener blade.

42

Uncle Ev's face lit up. "Sammy, do you think you can?"

She took the canteen and pried at it. Money in a canteen, in a meadow at dawn. It seemed entirely likely that Uncle Everett was cracking up.

She got part of the top cut away. Uncle Everett grabbed it eagerly. The ragged tin cut Sam's finger, but he didn't notice.

"Sammy," he said, "I always said you had a head on your shoulders." He was pulling out tightly folded bills, lots of them. "Yes, sir, a real head." He was smoothing out the money carefully and putting it into his pocket.

"It looks like a lot of money," Sam said.

"You said it, Sammy," he said. "Your old Uncle Ev isn't always such a dud."

"Is it all yours?"

He glanced at her sharply. "Of course it's all mine. I got lucky in a couple of games."

"Aunt Martha said you didn't gamble any more." Sam said.

"Look," he said, "she's only against it when I lose, see? She *thinks* she's against gambling because some jerk minister told her it was sinful."

"Is it?"

"Of course it isn't," he said indignantly. "How do you think Rockefeller and all those fellers made their pile?"

"I don't really know," Sam said.

"Brains and luck. They had it here." He tapped his forehead significantly. "When opportunity knocked, they opened the blasted door, that's all. Taking a chance. It's the American way."

It was something Sam would like to consider later,

but right now she was cold and her finger was bleeding rather badly.

He noticed the blood dripping on the snow. "Hey," he said, "you ought to take care of that."

"It's just a scratch," she said.

He shuddered and looked away. She remembered that blood made him sick. She wrapped her Kleenex around it and held it tight to slow down the bleeding.

"I owe you something, Sammy," he said. "You been real good."

"That's all right," Sam said. "Are you coming back to the house now? It's pretty cold."

He hesitated. "Can you keep a secret, Sammy?"

"Sure," Sam said.

"I'm going on a little trip."

"That's nice," she said. "Where to, Uncle Ev?"

He looked sideways at her. "What if I told you Paris, France?"

She forgot that she was cold and her finger hurt. Uncle Ev was going to get his big dream! "Maybe you'll get to Italy, too," she said, "and see the Leaning Tower of Pisa. . . ."

"Paris, France," he said, "is where I'm going."

"I guess Paris is pretty great, all right. Especially in the spring. I mean the way people write songs about it and everything."

"I'm going right now," he said. "In the fall."

"Well, that's great. I'm really pleased. And Aunt Martha will go out of it, won't she! She won't even mind about the gambling, I'll bet."

He frowned. "Sam . . ." He squinted his eyes and stared into the trees. "Sammy, you and me always been buddies, right?"

"Sure."

"OK. I'm going to count on you. I need your help, see? For reasons I can't go into right now, this has to be a secret. I mean right now, at this stage of things."

"You mean from everybody?"

"Everybody." He studied her. "You said you could keep a secret. Just for a little while, you know."

"Yes, I promised."

He patted her shoulder. "You're a good kid. And you done me a real favor, opening that canteen. I'm going to see to it that you get your heart's desire. You remember that day we talked about heart's desires and stuff like that?"

"Yes," Sam said.

"Well, you're going to get your Christmas present early. How about that?"

"You don't have to do anything like that," Sam said. Maybe he meant to get her another cashmere. There was this girl at school who had thirty-one cashmere sweaters, all different colors. Sam had heard a girl who had seen them say so, so it was true.

He clapped his hands like a delighted child. "Guess what you're going to get."

"Another sweater?" When he shook his head, she said, "A pair of racing skates?"

"Nah," he said scornfully. "No skates. I'm going to give you what you really want. I'm going to get you one of them puppies."

Sam felt the blood rush to her face. "What puppies?" she said faintly.

"Them Russian dogs you set such store by."

"Irish," she said. "Irish." She repeated it softly as if it were a holy word.

"That's it. What did your dad say that guy's name was?"

"McDermott. Ask at Pete's place." She didn't dare believe it. "Uncle Ev, they cost an awful lot."

He waved his hand. "Forget it. I repay favors."

"An Irish wolfhound. Oh, Uncle Ev—" Her eyes filled with tears.

"Here, here," he said, pleased. "None of that."

"But an Irish wolfhound, just because I opened a canteen?"

"And because you're going to keep quiet about it for a day or so. Agreed?" He zipped up the pocket in his jacket that held the money. It bulged. "Now you scuttle on home and tell the folks I'll be out hunting a spell longer." He winked at her. "Got to go into town and make some arrangements."

"OK," Sam said. She had a vision of travelers' checks and passports, and Uncle Everett coming home for dinner and springing his big surprise on everybody. And perhaps bringing her dog right then, if Mr. McDermott had one that he wanted to sell. "Do you want me to run you over in the boat?"

"No, no," he said quickly. "I'll use the crossover up at the end of the island. Your dad might want the outboard before I get back." He gave her a gay little wave. "So long, Sammy."

"So long." Sam watched him go. He plodded along looking like the squat little Aztec god her father had a carving of. Then she put that thought out of her mind because it was unflattering to Uncle Everett, who had just become the greatest benefactor of her life.

It was a waiting kind of day. The moisture from
the early morning rain slipped down black tree trunks
in quivering pendant shapes, and smoky tail ends of cloud
hung in the sky.

In the laundry Babe looked often out of the window
as she sorted the clothes for the washing machine. "It's
no day to dry," she said to Albert as he came through
the laundry on his way to his workshop.

Sam sat on the floor holding her guinea pig. She was
worried about Uncle Ev. He had been gone a long time.

"I wonder what's keeping Everett out so long," Babe
said.

"He's probably holed up with a thermos of coffee and
a good book." Albert laughed. "I wonder if Ev has ever
read a good book."

Babe frowned. "He doesn't know anything about the
woods. He could get lost."

"We go through this every year," Albert said. "Ev

won't get lost. He has his own special gods looking after him." He went on into the workshop and soon the thin whine of the electric saw cut a jagged pattern in the stillness.

Babe went into the kitchen and made cocoa for Sam and herself. They sat at the kitchen table to drink it. The clock that looked like a blue willowware plate said four-thirty.

"It's much too late," Babe said. "On a day like this, the dark comes fast. If Everett isn't back by the time we finish the cocoa, we're all going to look for him."

Sam stirred her cocoa, spooning off the skim of milk on the top. She felt terrible, knowing where Uncle Ev had gone and just sitting there letting her mother worry. But she had promised. Besides, knowing where he had gone was not knowing where he was now. She was worried, herself. He could have gone to town and back three times in the length of time since she had seen him set out.

Attracted by the smell of cocoa Aunt Martha wandered downstairs. She was wearing a kelly green quilted bathrobe and she had her hair done up in fat plastic curlers. They pulled her hair back from her forehead, making it pink and shiny.

"Ev not back yet?" she said. She sat down and accepted the cocoa and cake that Babe offered her.

"He'll be along soon," Babe said.

"I could go look for him," Sam said.

Babe glanced at her quickly. "If he doesn't come in a little while, you and your father might go out to the meadow and get him. He must be soaking wet."

"You make lovely cocoa, Babe," Aunt Martha said dreamily.

Mark came in the back door. "Isn't Uncle Ev back yet?"

Babe got up. "Call your father, Sam, please."

Sam went to get her father. With every minute she felt worse about not telling them. When they were back in the kitchen, Martha looked at them.

"What's the matter," she said. "Are you afraid Everett is lost?" She half rose from the table. "It's almost dark out. He must be lost."

"Now, now," Albert said. "Of course not. But we'll go take a look." He began pulling on his storm boots that had been drying besides the stove. "He probably shot one of my sheep by mistake," he said, trying to sound as if he were joking, "and he's afraid to come home."

"I was out to the north meadow," Mark said. "I didn't see him."

"It's easy to get mixed up on those trails," Albert said.

"Why don't you build a big bonfire in the meadow?" Babe said. "Sam, you can tend it while Mark and your father and I hunt. Everett will certainly see it, even if he is lost."

"Good idea," Albert said. "But Babe, you stay here and if Ev shows up here first, give a blast with the .22."

"What about me?" Martha said. "He's my husband."

"You'll have to keep me company," Babe said. "I'm scared of guns."

"*You*'re scared of guns," Martha said.

"Take plenty of matches," Babe said to Albert. "And the flash and the Coleman lantern. They're there on the shelf under the nails."

Aunt Martha began to weep. "Those bears and wolves and things will get him."

"Nonsense," Albert said. "He's safe as if he were home in bed."

They put on heavy sweaters and raincoats and boots, and Sam took the Winchester. She didn't want to stay and guard the fire. She was nervous now, and she wanted to search, especially in the area where she had discovered Uncle Everett that morning.

But her father insisted that she stay with the fire. He got it going for her and then he and Mark cut off at different angles, one across the meadow, one into the woods.

Sam kicked up the edge of the fire until the flames shot up. Wherever you are, Uncle Ev, she prayed, come on in. She checked the gun to make sure it was loaded. She hoped her mother would not have to use hers.

The waiting was hard. She sat down after a while and watched the fire flicker lazily against the darkness that fell quickly. It would be terrible if something happened to Uncle Ev just when he had his dream in the palm of his hand. And her dream, too. The wolfhound was more than a dog. She saw herself traveling around the world exhibiting the Irish she had raised. It seemed like a lovely way of life. And she would see all the places she had read about.

She got up and threw more wood on the fire. She found a jagged rock to lean against, and she tipped her head back to look at the stars. But the grass and pine needles under her were wet, and the stars looked cold and distant. She concentrated on following Uncle Ev in her imagination. He had gone up to the end of the island and crossed over to the mainland. It would take him maybe twenty minutes to walk into town. Then what? There was no travel bureau that she knew of. Maybe he telephoned one. Would they be open on Saturday? What about passports? There was probably quite a lot to do if you were planning to go to Paris. He would have to buy luggage. The more she thought about it, the more likely it seemed that these things would take a long time. And yet, he hated the dark. She couldn't imagine his returning to the island on foot after dark.

She decided to think about something else. Maybe that would make him come back sooner. She would think about Miss Barracini. Miss Barracini. Angela Barracini. It was a strange and pretty name. It made Sam think of floating in a gondola. People said that Miss Barracini had been a cellist in a symphony orchestra somewhere, but she had to give it up and teach because her father died and she had to support some younger sister in a boarding school. That was a nice thing to do all right, but it didn't seem altogether right to Sam. A person should be very careful of a talent. She wished she knew Miss Barracini better. She was very beautiful, like an old Italian painting.

The sad howl of a coyote brought her to her feet. Her mind had been wandering, and the fire was sputtering. She picked out a couple of big limbs and tossed them into the flickering flames.

She knelt watching the fire, thinking of fire and the way it was both constant and changing. It was like the things that happened to you, changing all the time and yet becoming a permanent part of you. It was hard to understand. Anyway the fire would look good to Uncle Ev. She remembered how scared he had been in the woods the night before, even when they were with him. It was strange the things that frightened people. It would never occur to her to be afraid of the woods unless she met some real danger, but every day of her life she was afraid to go to school. And Uncle Ev, who was afraid of a snowy owl, could sail off to Paris without a second thought. And he could ride from Butte to Missoula on the train for years, collecting tickets from perfect strangers and talking to them as if it were nothing.

She turned her head quickly at the sound of a faint rustle. A mother skunk and three young skunks paused at the edge of the firelight, looked at her curiously, and marched off in single file like a mother and her children going to church.

Sam stretched out on her stomach close to the fire. She liked to feel the strong heat on her face while the sharp night air nipped at her legs. She hoped Uncle Everett was warm. To pass the time she began to conjugate irregular verbs for Monday's test. Thanks to her father's strict training before she and Mark went to the public school, she had been getting *A*'s but she wasn't sure she could keep it up. There were some smart people in her class. She wished she could get to know them more easily. They had gone through all those years of school together, and they didn't need her. And there were so many things they knew that she didn't know. Like how to apply eye shadow.

A faint sound made her turn her head. On the farthest rim of the circle of firelight stood a timber wolf. The drift of the smoke was in his nostrils. Sam reached for her gun. He was magnificent—tensed, gaunt-framed, and big. His eyes were shining yellow in the firelight. She hated killing game but a wolf is destructive. Last winter a wolf, perhaps this one, had found her pet lamb and left him a mass of bloody bones. And a wolf had raided the hen house several times. She took careful aim.

"*Lupus, benedictus est,*" she murmured, and tensed her finger on the trigger. But she did not fire the gun. There was a faint single report of a .22 in the distance. The wolf heard it too, and melted into the night.

She lay still for a moment, relieved that she had not had to kill the wolf. The signal had come from her mother, probably indicating that Uncle Ev was safe at home. She jumped up and began to stamp out the fire.

Mark arrived and then her father. They carried water from the creek in a battered pail that Albert had brought. Mark and Sam doused the flames, and Albert stamped out the last of the sparks with his heavy boots.

Albert led the way home. The wavering light of the lantern splashed down on his head like a slippery halo. A short way behind him came Mark, the steady gleam of his torch angled downward.

The lonely howl of a wolf etched the stillness. Sam wondered if it was her wolf. Something would have to be done, of course. There wasn't room on the island for both wolves and ranchers. She knew it, but it made her sad.

The stars were gone now and a slow, bone-chilling rain dripped through the trees. The darkness seemed to have height and weight. Ahead of her a dead bough caught against her father's arm and broke with a crack like a gunshot. The black, wet trees crowded in on her, slowing her down. Water that had worked its way into her boots squished uncomfortably. Buck brush caught at the tin pail in her hand and sent it clattering.

"This damnable night!" Albert said. "It's black as pitch."

As they came into the clearing near the house, they became aware of a muffled wail.

"It's Martha!" Albert began to run.

The house seemed to jump at them, ablaze with lights. Babe opened the door as they ran up the steps.

In the hall Martha was leaning back in a chair, a wad of wet Kleenex in her lap. Her makeup was tracked with tears.

"What's wrong?" Albert said.

Sam seized her mother's arm. "Uncle Ev?"

Aunt Martha burst into a new attack of sobbing.

Mark took the lantern from his father and blew out the pale flame.

"Western Union called," Babe said. She looked at the piece of paper in her hand as if she were not quite sure how it got there. She read it:

" 'Ran into old buddy. Offered me fabulous deal. Had to leave at once to clinch it. Letter follows. Cheerio. Ev.' "

Albert pushed back the hair from his forehead. "For the love of heaven," he said, "I thought he was dead or something. Cheerio, indeed."

"He's left me," Martha wailed. "I know it." She peered blearily at Albert.

"That's nonsense," he said, "and you know it. If the man has a chance to make some money, you ought to be rejoicing, not bawling. You know how Ev is about his 'little deals.' "

"He's left me," Martha moaned. "He's run off with some floozy."

Albert sat down and tugged at his boots. "Nuts," he said. "Ev doesn't have it in him. But I wish he had let us know. It's cold in those woods."

"Mark," Babe said, "help your aunt upstairs."

Martha lurched to her feet, and leaned heavily on

Mark's reluctant arm.

"I'll bring you some hot chocolate," Babe said. "It will help you sleep. And you're not to worry, Martha."

Albert and Babe went into the living room, and Sam followed them. "That nutty brother of yours," Albert said.

Babe shook her head. "Something is wrong."

"Nothing except that Ev is up to one of his little deals."

Sam felt angry with her father for his easy dismissal of things. "Something *is* wrong," she said.

Babe looked at her quickly. "What is it?"

She told them what had happened that morning.

Albert was furious. "In the name of heaven, why didn't you tell us? We spent the whole lousy night prowling in the cold. . ."

"I promised not to tell for a day or so," Sam said. "I guess the day is up now."

"Did you know he wasn't coming back?" Babe asked.

"No, Mother, I told you. I thought he had just gone into town for an hour or so, about tickets and stuff. I thought he might really be lost."

"He's ditched Martha," Albert said. "Dumped her on us."

"I'm sure he hasn't," Sam said. "I'm sure he'll send for her."

"Of course he will," Babe said. But she had a worried little frown.

"You and your relatives," Albert said. "That's what comes of messing around with other people."

"He's our uncle," Sam said. "He's Mom's brother."

"Uncle. He's a nuisance and a nut." Albert slammed out of the room.

SAM CUT GYM ON MONDAY. WITHOUT EVER QUITE SAYING
so, she and Miss Barracini had arrived at an understand-
ing. Instead of going to gym, Sam went to the little
room where Miss Barracini kept the music and records
and the record player. For a happy hour Sam played
records, the volume turned very low, while in the next
room Miss Barracini gave a cello lesson, and outside the
window Sam's classmates shrieked and collided with each
other and bumped a volleyball from one side of the net
to the other. The gym teacher, who never took roll, had
not commented on Sam's absences.

Today Sam looked through the records. She was
developing a fondness for Vivaldi, Corelli, Palestrina, and
Bach. It was music with a pattern that she could follow.

Carefully she lifted a Vivaldi from its cover and
placed it on the turntable. She lay on the floor to listen.
Part of her mind followed the music carefully and part
of it kept coming back to Uncle Everett. His strange dis-

appearance troubled her. She could not understand at all why he had left without a word and why he had lied in the telegram. Perhaps he was making arrangements for the trip to Paris and was going to surprise Aunt Martha, but why had he left so suddenly? She closed her eyes and saw Uncle Everett in hunting clothes, his gun over his shoulder and his knapsack full of money, strolling down the Champs Elysees, bowing and smiling. But surely he wouldn't go without Aunt Martha.

For a moment a lifting phrase of music caught her whole attention, and the image of Uncle Everett vanished. The door opened. It was Miss Barracini. Politely Sam got to her feet, but Miss Barracini waved her hand impatiently. "Don't interrupt the *Pastorale Dance*." She sank down on the floor beside Sam. Her scarlet peasant skirt billowed out around her. She sat cross-legged, elbows on knees, and listened with completely absorbed attention.

Sam watched her. Miss Barracini was unlike anyone she had ever seen. She was always changing, sometimes silent as if her thoughts were thousands of miles away, sometimes vivacious and talkative, sometimes cool and watchful.

As the music ended, she looked up and gave Sam a brilliant smile. "It's nice that you come here to listen," she said. "Most of them prefer rock and roll."

"Rock and roll makes the inside of my stomach jump," Sam said.

Miss Barracini laughed.

Shyly Sam said, "I never knew a musician before."

"Musicians." Miss Barracini shrugged. "Some so-called musicians have no more feeling for music than a cow. They have a certain dexterity with the fingers and an ability to read notes." She got up and changed the record. The opening bars of a Bach violin concerto filled the room. She stretched out on the sofa with the creaking springs, her arms under her head, her eyes closed.

Sam tilted her head so that she could look out the window. Her father told her once that only a device in the eye made human beings see the world in the way that they called 'right side up,' and that some people who didn't have this device saw it upside down. She narrowed her eyes and imagined that the thick clay-colored sky was a floor, with the trees stuck up like black-stemmed mushrooms. She imagined the volleyball going down instead of up, and the girls bumping and rushing around the court on their heads, with their legs thrashing foolishly in the air. She laughed.

Miss Barracini opened her eyes, startled. Sam shook her head apologetically and turned her gaze toward the real floor. Miss Barracini was watching her and it made her nervous. She hadn't meant to laugh aloud. She hated to have people think she was odd, especially Miss Barracini. But she couldn't very well explain that she had laughed at the world being upside down.

The graceful dignity of the Andante caught her attention and she lay still, listening. As the sunny Allegro began, she looked up and exchanged a delighted smile with Miss Barracini.

The brutal clang of the class bell made them both jump. Sam got to her feet reluctantly.

"Can't you stay?" Miss Barracini said.

"I have algebra," Sam said.

"I'll explain to Mr. Stone," Miss Barracini said. "Do stay." She smiled with such warmth that Sam felt a little dizzy.

Sam felt the gritty dust of the record cabinet under her fingers. Behind her, around her, the music picked out its serene and delicate path. Against the sound of the music she heard the thud of students' feet pounding by outside the window, and padding by in the corridor.

"Stay," Miss Barracini said.

Sam nodded happily, and at Miss Barracini's gesture she sat on the floor by the couch. Miss Barracini lit a cigarette and sank back on the couch. Sam watched the thin smoke curl up in slow spirals above their heads. It was against the rules for anyone, even teachers, to smoke in the building. It made Sam feel pleasantly excited that she and Miss Barracini were breaking rules together.

Neither of them moved or spoke until the music came to an end. Sam had the feeling that she had not even breathed. Miss Barracini sat up and put out her cigarette, grinding it into the coffee can that she used as an ash tray. The paper split and the brown shreds of tobacco spilled out in a little heap. It was strange about rules, Sam thought. What harm could it do anyone if Miss Barracini had a cigarette or if she cut algebra to listen to Bach? Rules were hateful. It was different on the island, where the only rules were the ones that had a clear and sensible purpose, like remembering to feed the stock and milk the cow. In that moment Sam felt that she understood perfectly why her father had chosen to live on the island.

"I wish you could see our island," she said.

Miss Barracini was taking the record off the turn-table. She did not speak until she had placed it carefully inside its plastic protector and in its album.

"The island where you live?" she said. "I'd like to sometime." She put the album in the cabinet. "Only two of Bach's violin concertos have survived. We know that he wrote others because we have the versions transcribed for the clavier but the original manuscripts were lost." She sounded like a teacher now.

Without the music the room seemed different. Smaller and dreary and dusty. Outside the gray sky pressed down upon the earth.

"Thank you ever so much," Sam said, and left.

"What is a clavier?" Sam asked.

"Some kind of old piano, I think," Babe said. "Ask your father. You're late getting home."

"I was kept after," Sam said.

"Whatever for? Your father wants you to go with him when he takes Aunt Martha to the bus."

"I didn't know she was going. Has anything happened?" She searched her mother's face.

"No. But she wants to go home. I urged her to stay. It isn't easy for her to take care of herself—" She paused worriedly. "I just can't imagine what's got into Everett." She pushed the hair back from her forehead. "Why did you have to stay after school?"

"I cut algebra class," Sam said. And then she added, "and gym."

"How did you happen to do that?"

"Well, I was listening to some records and Miss Barracini said why didn't I stay a little longer—so I did."

"Then why didn't Miss what's-her-name give you an excuse or something?"

"She was going to explain to the teacher. I guess she forgot."

"Why didn't *you* explain?"

Sam looked shocked. "I couldn't do that."

"Why not? Why did you let a misunderstanding like that put you in a bad light?"

"It wasn't really important," Sam said. "Kids stay after school all the time."

"Well, my children don't," Babe said. "I'm not going to have those teachers think my children don't know right from wrong. If you won't tell him, I'll just write him a note myself."

Sam was horrified. "Mother, you wouldn't!"

"I certainly would." Babe's mouth trembled. "We were brought up to do right in our family. My brother Everett knows. . . ." Her eyes filled with tears and she turned away.

Sam was astonished. She could count on one hand the number of times she had seen her mother cry. And what did Uncle Everett have to do with her cutting algebra? Then it came to her that her mother was worrying about Uncle Everett, not really about her. There had been no word from him since the telegram.

"Mother," she said gently. She reached out her hand, not quite touching her. "Mom—"

"I'll just write that teacher a note," Babe said. She burst into tears and left the room.

Sam went outside and sat on the edge of the swimming pool. She gazed at the swirl of dead leaves beneath her feet. She could not understand why Uncle Everett had not gotten in touch with them, why he had not made arrangements for Aunt Martha to join him. Even getting passports couldn't take this long, and anyway he could call up. She didn't understand why he had led her to think he was coming back that day when she had found him in the meadow. The only answers that came to her were not ones that she wanted to believe.

Babe had told Aunt Martha some of what Sam had told her parents. First Aunt Martha had shrieked that she was deserted, and then she had done a turnabout and announced that of course Ev would send for her.

"He's just like a kid about surprises," she said. "He's getting everything in order. Oh, we'll have a lovely time!" And she asked Sam to get a travel book on France at the library.

Then she decided to return to Butte and pack her things. They were waiting now for Albert to come home, to take Martha into town to the bus station.

Sam hoped Uncle Everett would not be angry with her for telling. She had waited as long as she could. Surely he would understand. She pictured him walloping her on the back and saying, 'Of course you done the right thing, Sammy.'

Her father arrived and together they carried Aunt Martha's heavy suitcases to the boat. "Martha," he grumbled, "what do you pack in these things—bricks?" He was tired. He had been climbing around in the rugged Mission mountains near St. Ignatius, looking at a mine that some man was interested in. Although it was a long time since his own mining days, he still acted as a consultant now and then. He was known in the area for his skill in assessing a mine's potential. Sometimes he took Sam with him, but nowadays school interfered with such pleasant trips.

"Wait till I'm packed to go to Paris," Aunt Martha was saying. "It'll take ten porters. And when I get there. . ." She sighed dreamily. "Paris clothes, perfume, all kinds of stuff."

"Martha," Albert said, "don't count on it. It might

not work out. It takes a lot of money to go to Europe."

"Ev will take care of it," Martha said.

Her father said no more. On the far side of the river he reached for their dock and jumped out, fastening the boat chain to the dock's iron ring. He reached down into the boat to help Aunt Martha, as she made her lunge for the dock. For a moment Sam thought Aunt Martha's bulk had carried Albert clear off the other side of the dock but there was no splash. Then she heard him say, "Hurry up, Sam, or we'll miss the stupid bus."

Sam could tell by the way he gunned the engine of the pickup that he was really anxious to get rid of Aunt Martha. Sam was squeezed tight between them and it was hard to keep her legs out of the way of the gears.

Her father started up too jerkily and the engine stalled.

"Won't it go?" Aunt Martha asked.

When her father didn't answer, Sam said, "It always does that when it's cold. We need a new distributor or something."

"Well, goodness," Aunt Martha said, "you ought to get that fixed, Albert. Everett always says a car is like a train—if it won't run, what good is it?"

Albert pumped the gas pedal and the engine roared. "Everett," he said, "speaks with the tongue of angels."

When they reached the station and Aunt Martha's baggage was stowed away in the great belly of the bus, and she herself was about to be swallowed up by the monster, Sam felt such a wrench of pity for her that if Albert had not grabbed her arm, she would have jumped in after Aunt Martha just so she wouldn't feel alone.

The driver started the wheezing mechanism that closed the door. She could see Aunt Martha's fat cheek pressed against the tiny window, and one plump hand raised in farewell. Then the great gray whale spewed forth a sickening smoke and floated down the street.

They walked down the main street toward the Last Chance Bar and Grille. A busy autumn wind slapped dry leaves against the store fronts and around their feet. Clouds like torn grey rags raced across the face of the setting sun, turning everything murky. As the sun began its slow slide below the horizon, there was a kind of coppery half-light. Sam felt as if she were looking through dirty yellow sun glasses.

"The weather is up to something," Albert said, "darned if I know what."

They passed the public telephone booth standing empty in the middle of a vacant lot. Albert kicked aside a beer can that was in his way, and it rattled tinnily across the hard ground. On the far side of the vacant lot Sam could see a light in the high school. The janitor probably or some teacher working late. Or Miss Barracini playing the cello. Sam and Mark had stopped outside the school one evening to listen. She played beautifully. The rich, full melody had sounded strange coming from that ugly, empty building at night.

They ducked their heads as the wind slapped dust in their faces. An old newspaper wrapped around Sam's legs. She stopped to pull it loose. They were in front of the Mercantile now, and she leaned against the window to look at a display of skirts and sweaters. The Back to School sign was still there, a little fly-specked. "Make the scholar in your house happy in a Penworthy twin set." And above the sign there was a pen-and-ink sketch of a girl's face smiling vacuously. Sam pressed her cheek against the window. Her vague feeling of depression grew stronger.

"This is a great time to window-shop," Albert said impatiently.

She caught up with him. "Did you know," she said morosely, "that the kick pleat in front is out?"

"The what?"

"Kick pleat. The only skirt I ever really liked is that yellowy tweed one that you got me in Victoria."

"That English material is very good," he said. "I got a jacket there twelve or fourteen years ago. It's still good."

"I've had this skirt three years," Sam said.

"So?" He took her arm, to hurry her along.

"I wore it to school and felt funny in it. Some of the girls stared."

"For heaven's sake, why?"

"The kick pleat is in front," she said dismally.

He looked astonished and then he laughed. "That must be what is known as planned obsolescence."

"I don't know what it's known as," she said, "but I know what I'm known as. A hick."

"Save it for another year," he said. "It will come back in style."

"But I won't," she said. It seemed to her that he was being very unfeeling. "I'll never be in style because I don't know anything."

He stopped and looked at her. "Baby," he said, "are you serious?"

"Yes," she said emphatically. "I'm Out. I'm some nut or something from an island."

"Honey," he said, "those things aren't important."

"They are to me," she said.

He frowned. 'Haven't I taught you any sense of

values? You know things that really matter. You can quote John Donne, you know a little Greek, you can identify rotifers, you know the habits of the trumpeter swan . . ."

"But I don't know about kick pleats," she said. "And I've never been to a football game."

"Well!" he said, "you *are* in a black mood. What you need is a good, juicy hamburger." They walked diagonally across the street toward the Grille.

The sky was darkening and lights were going on in houses on adjacent streets. The neon lights at the Last Chance Bar and Grille flickered sickly. Some of the letters failed to light up, so that the sign read L-ST C-A-NCE BA- AND GRILLE. Someone in a noisy, old Ford drove up in front of the place and went in.

A gust of wind caught Albert's battered Stetson and skimmed it along the sidewalk. It flattened against the front of J.C. Penney's, where it beat like a trapped bird.

"Go ahead," Sam said. "I'll get it." As she reached Penney's, the wind snatched the hat out of reach. "Come here, stupid," she said. She pounced on it and caught the brim.

She straightened up. Her father's tall figure was silhouetted against the light that crept through and over the swinging doors at the Last Chance. He was waiting for her, and she could see the tension of impatience and hunger in the way he stood. She started toward him.

Crossing the alley that ran parallel to the building, she glanced down it because alleys always fascinated her. In this one there was the usual collection of trash cans, empty cardboard cartons, and trash, heaped up around the back door of the Last Chance.

Sam stopped dead and her knees began to shake.

66

Standing close to the trash cans there stood a white, Irish wolfhound. He stood motionless and alert. In the dark and dirty alley, he gleamed palely like a great ghost of a dog. Sam dropped her father's hat and moved slowly toward the dog.

Her father called to her impatiently. When she didn't answer, he came to see what was wrong. The heels of his boots made a tat-tat-tat in the silence. He came into the alley and stopped.

"It must be one of McDermott's dogs," he said, after a moment.

"It's mine," Sam said. She didn't know why she was so sure, but she was.

"Don't be silly," Albert said. "I told you, we can't afford a dog like that." When she said nothing, he said, "Come on, let's see if we can get something to eat. I'm starved."

"I'll come in a minute," Sam said. "I want to look at the dog a little while."

"Sam . . ." Her father looked at her face. "Well, all right. I'll call you when the hamburgers are ready. Do you want everything on yours?"

She nodded, not taking her eyes off the dog.

"Don't get too close to him," Albert said. "He might be mean."

She looked at him with such reproach that he laughed. "Just the same, be careful." He turned up the collar of his jacket and headed back to the Grille.

Slowly Sam moved closer to the dog. She would not go right up to him, since her father had said not to. She spoke to him in a low voice. "Hi, boy. How are you, boy?"

The dog cocked his big head and looked at her questioningly. His great yellow eyes were soft in the half-dark. His curly, coarse white coat clung to his big-boned body. He looked not quite full grown, although he stood more than three feet at the withers. There was still a puppy look about him.

The door of the cafe opened and shut and she heard her father and someone else coming up behind her.

"It's hers, all right," a man's voice said. He went up to the dog and put his hand on the flat part of the dog's head, between the ears.

Over the pounding of her heart Sam heard her father say, "McDermott, are you sure?"

McDermott squatted down beside the dog and rolled a cigarette. The cloth of his blue jeans, worn to a velvet smoothness, contrasted with the elegant pearl-buttoned shirt, the string tie, and the expensive Stetson shoved onto the back of his head. He had a long, leathery face with squinted, pale eyes that looked past people when he talked.

"I thought you'd be a boy," he said to Sam. "This little guy come by and give me money, cash on the line. 'Take that dog out to the Daley island,' he said, 'and deliver it to Sam.'"

Sam moved closer to the dog. She knelt so that her eyes were on a level with his. She reached out and touched one of his long ears.

"Careful," her father said sharply.

"No need to be careful," McDermott said. "Irish are gentlemen." He rubbed the top of the dog's head.

"How old is he?" Albert asked.

"Almost nine months. Just about got his growth. But he's still a mite awkward."

"I should hope so," Albert said. "He must be three

feet tall."

"A wee bit over." McDermott smiled.

"Eats like a horse, no doubt."

"They're not what you'd call picky eaters," McDermott said.

Sam rocked back on her heels, never taking her eyes off the dog. He was lying down now, hind legs sprawled out, his head on his huge front paws, studying Sam.

"This man who bought the dog," Albert said. "What was his name?"

McDermott shrugged. "I don't recall. He gave me cash, and the place of delivery." He rummaged in his jeans pocket until he found a scrap of paper. He squinted at it and then handed it to Albert. "I'll send you the papers as soon as I get home. They don't come any better stock. I hope you'll show him."

Albert struck a match and looked at the paper. "It's Everett's writing."

Sam was afraid to look at her father. She touched the dog's coat, feeling the soft, coarse hair and the strong bones underneath.

"He must have been out of his mind," Albert said. "I have no use for a monster like this."

Gently McDermott said, "T'is not you he gave it to, Mr. Daley, no offense."

Albert looked startled for a moment.

"And besides," McDermott said, "begging to disagree, I think you do have a need for him. You have wolves on your island."

"That's right," Sam said, her voice breaking a little in her anxiety. "I saw a wolf myself, out in the meadow."

"And a good watch dog he'll be," McDermott went on in his quiet voice. "For the missus."

"I thought you said they were gentle," Albert said.

"And that they are. But nobody's going to fool with a dog this big, Mr. Daley. And they'll protect their own. Grab my arm." He thrust out his skinny forearm. "Go on, man, grab it."

Albert seized McDermott's wrist. Almost before he had completed the motion the dog was on his feet growling.

McDermott put his hand on the dog's back. "It's all right, boy." And to Albert he said, "You see?"

"How much does a dog like this cost?" Albert asked.

"He was four hundred dollars. Your little friend beat me down some."

"Why on earth would Everett spend all that money?" Albert said to Sam.

Sam interrupted her father quickly. "What is the dog's name, Mr. McDermott?"

"This dog's name is Cormac," McDermott said. "He's named for a king of Ireland, fourth century. Come inside and I'll tell you a tale or two about the Irish." He untied the dog's chain and handed it to Sam. "Bring the dog with you."

Inside the warm little cafe Cormac lay at Sam's feet filling the space between the counter and the booths. No one else except the counterman was in the cafe. He leaned over the counter to admire the dog. "Big brute, ain't he," he said.

"Too big," Albert grumbled. "And too valuable for a kid to own."

McDermott pushed the sugar bowl toward Sam. "Put plenty of sugar in your coffee, child. A growing girl needs energy." He took out an oddly carved pipe and lit it carefully. "Now about these dogs. We have the first written record of the Irish in the second century after the birth of Christ. The Celts—my ancestors and his . . ." He touched Cormac's head. " . . . took their hounds to Greece when they made war. Two hundred years later we find a letter from a Roman big shot, a congressman, like, thanking his brother for seven Irish wolfhounds. Fought them in the circus. And in the tenth century there's a Norwegian prince. . . ." McDermott paused and searched through his wallet until he found a scrap of paper with neat handwriting on it "Olaf, his name was, and he turned up in one of them Norway sagas and he says, 'I will give thee a hound . . .' " McDermott twisted around on his seat so that the paper was under the light. " '. . . that was given to me in Ireland; he is big, and no worse than a stout man. Besides it is part of his nature that he has a man's wit and he will bay at every man whom he knows to be thy foe, but never at thy friends. He can see, too, in any man's face whether he means thee well or ill, and he will lay down his life to be true to thee. This hound's name is Sam.' "

"Sam!" Sam wheeled around on the stool so abruptly that she almost fell off.

"Come on, McDermott," Albert said, "don't pull the kid's leg."

McDermott fixed his small, pale eyes on Albert with a detached look. "You are an educated man," he said. "Look it up in the university library at Missoula. *The Saga of Burnt Njal*, it's called. Or you'll find as much as I just read in the *AKC Dog Book*." He finished his coffee in one long swallow and slid off the stool. The dog got to his feet. McDermott took Sam's hand and placed it on the dog's muzzle. "Stay, boy. Stay, Cormac," he said. He left some money on the counter for the coffee and walked out of the cafe without another word.

"Pete," Albert said, "you know this guy better than I do. Is he a nut?"

"I should be such a nut," Pete said. He mopped the counter with a wet rag. "He's a real smart guy. Knows dogs. He makes a good living off them big hounds. Sells them to ranchers a lot, and ships them back East and California and all over. You got a good dog there, Sam, a real good dog."

"I know," Sam said softly.

"If I decide to give the dog back, where does McDermott live?" Albert said.

"Helena. But you'd be crazy to give back a dog like that."

Albert looked at the dog and then at Sam. "Oh," he said, "let's go home. We can worry about this tomorrow."

Sam let out her breath. "Come on, Cormac."

The dog moved beside her with easy grace. Sam felt as though she were striding across the green countryside of Ireland in seven-league boots.

Babe was upset. "Ev shouldn't have done that. It was like a bribe."

"He said it was an early Christmas present."

"For keeping your mouth shut till he got out of town," Albert said.

"But I told you, I didn't know he was leaving town."

"He's too big a dog for the house," Babe said. "I guess you can keep him in the barn for now."

Sam left quickly for the barn before her mother should define 'for now.' Mark helped her pitch clean hay into an empty box stall. Cormac wandered around making cautious acquaintance with the horses, cattle, and sheep. "He's careful with the stock," Mark said. "That's good."

The two border collies trotted in to inspect the newcomer. Cormac was eager to play but after a critical sniffing, they left again. Sam leaned on the pitchfork and watched Cormac. He nuzzled the Jersey heifer, who turned her head to gaze at him with limpid eyes. Her creamy coat was just a shade darker than his. He ducked as the heifer lowered her head and butted.

Mark laughed but Sam comforted Cormac. "She's just a dumb old cow." She stroked his rough head.

"She was only being friendly," Mark said. He spread out a burlap bag for Cormac's bed.

The dog continued his tour. Some of the sheep, penned in for the night, huddled together as he approached them. They lifted their heads and rested their chins on each other's necks. A black-muzzled wether stamped the straw-strewn floor with his sharp hoofs, sending up a little cloud of chaff and dust. Cormac put his front paws on the gate and hunched his rear leg muscles for a spring.

"Down, Cormac!" Mark slapped his hands together sharply, and the dog dropped his feet to the floor.

"You didn't have to yell at him," Sam said.

"If he's going to live here, he's got to behave," Mark said. He patted the dog's shaggy neck. "Good boy."

"He's just come, for Pete's sake," Sam said. "Give him time."

"He has to learn from the start," Mark said sternly. "It's going to be tough enough to get Mother and Dad to let him stay. If he causes trouble, he won't have a chance."

"You don't have to be so bossy," Sam said. "He's not your dog." She was instantly ashamed, but she couldn't think what to say.

Mark looked hurt. He left the barn without a word.

"Mark," she called. "Mark, wait a minute—"

There was no answer. And in a moment she heard the kitchen door open and close. She was sorry that she

74

had been so disagreeable. She ought to go tell him; but she had decided to stay all night in the barn with Cormac, and when he came up and pushed his cold muzzle into her hand, she forgot about Mark.

When she awoke, she could see polka dots of milky white sky through the knotholes above her head. Dim and far in another world the early sounds of morning filtered into the barn. Someone had put a blanket around her during the night. She pulled it up. Cormac lay stretched out beside her, one forepaw touching her arm. He slept lightly, half-opening his amber eyes when she stirred. She put out her hand and touched him. He was real.

The horses were stomping and puffing with early morning restlessness, and the heifer raised her foolish head and mooed. As if in echo Sam heard the first notes of Mark's French horn. Mark had a knack for playing wind instruments with little instruction. He had just been assigned to the school band, and he was trying out the tune of the school's alma mater. There was a football game Friday night, and he would be playing.

"Did you ever see a football game?" Sam said to Cormac. He lifted his head and looked at her sleepily. "I never did either, and I'm almost sixteen years old. Can you believe it?" She sat up and brushed the straw from her jacket. Her legs were stiff from sleeping on the floor. She stretched.

Cormac scrambled to his feet and pushed his head against her. He caught her off balance and she nearly fell over backward. He leaned against her, nuzzling her roughly.

For a second she was frightened. He was so big. "Cormac!" she said sharply. "Stop it. Sit!"

Obediently he sat back on his haunches and looked at her mournfully. A good game spoiled.

"You play too rough," she said. "I'm not Mr. Mc-Dermott." She got up. "I'm going to train you. Starting right after school. First of all, no jumping and shoving—that'll get you fired out of here like a shot."

He followed her expectantly to the door.

"I suppose you're hungry," she said. She looked around the barn. "Not alfalfa, I guess. Nor oats." She poked around on the dusty shelves where odds and ends were stored. "Cat food. How about cat food?" She took down a big bag of kibble and poured some of it into a shallow pan.

Cormac took one enthusiastic mouthful and then drew back suspiciously.

"You have to wait then," she said. "We can't afford picky eaters around here." She left him in the barn and went to the house.

Her parents were talking in the kitchen. "As long as the dog is here," Babe was saying, "he'll have to stay. At least until we hear from Everett."

"But why did he give it to her? Well, I know why, but did it have to be a wolfhound? I'm not running a zoo."

Sam came in. "He knew I wanted one."

"So I want the Taj Mahal," Albert said. "I don't think even Ev will give it to me."

"He loves to give presents," Babe said. "He always has."

"We can't keep it."

Sam's stomach felt cold. "Why not?"

"It's a four-hundred-dollar dog."

"Albert," Babe said. "We'll have to think about it."

76

"He dumps Martha with us and bribes Sam and runs out. I don't like it."

"What would we do with Cormac then?" Sam's voice shook.

"We'll have to see," Babe said. "We'll have to think about it. If it's possible, your father will let you keep it, I think. It's only that it's so impractical—" Babe turned away from Sam's face.

"I was going to train him," Sam said. "He'll be the basis for my kennel. He'll really make money for us in the end. I mean I'd never be able to get a good dog like this myself—" She looked at her father.

Albert shrugged helplessly. "Maybe I can teach him to herd sheep."

Sam accepted it as giving in. She ran upstairs before he could change his mind.

The obedience book said that a half hour a day was enough for training, so Sam timed their daily practice carefully. Mr. McDermott had taught Cormac some of the basic commands. In the next few days, Sam rehearsed him in them until he was almost perfect.

"Stay!" she said to him, as Mark watched critically. Cormac hunched forward as if to follow her but he stayed. Sam walked some distance and then faced him. Cormac quivered with eagerness. "Stay!" she repeated. Then she brought her arm forward and sharply down. "Come!"

Cormac leaped toward her. On the "down" command, he flopped on his stomach, hind legs still erect.

"All the way down," she said, "Cormac, down."

Reluctantly he lowered his hind legs. She kept him in that position while she walked away. He inched forward a little, but when she faced him he sank down and

77

cocked his head. At the "come," he raced to her and bounded clumsily against her for the "heel" position. In his joy he knocked her down. She rolled on the ground laughing. Cormac accepted the slackening of discipline and together they wrestled in the frost-brown grass.

Mark came up to them. "He's getting better," he said, "but you shouldn't let him goof off."

Sam sat up gasping for breath. "He just got carried away. He's such a big nut." She hugged him and he lapped her neck in a delirium of joy.

Mark frowned. Dog training was serious business. But then Cormac put his huge paws on Mark's feet and looked up at him, one ear turned inside out and his mouth wide open in a panting grin. And Mark had to laugh, too. Sam caught him around the knees and pulled him down and the three of them thrashed around in a wild confusion.

That night at dinner Mark looked up casually and said, "Sam, how is Cormac's training coming along?"

Sam gave the prearranged answer. "Neat!" she said. "You ought to see him. Daddy, he's really smart."

Albert looked at them suspiciously

"Can you control him?" Mark asked her.

"Just about perfectly. Another few days and he'll be doing everything that obedience book says he should do."

"Have you spoken to him about giving up food?" Albert said. "I understand your whole week's allowance goes into dog food and knuckle bones."

"Well, we all have to eat," Sam said.

"Yes, but not necessarily a carload at a time. And what is this little act you and your brother just went through? Am I supposed to ask you when I can see this marvel of canine obedience?"

"Sam has worked hard, Dad," Mark said. "She's done a good job."

"Then why not just say so?" Albert said. "Why make a three-act play out of it?"

Sam didn't answer. She felt tired, and her father's sarcasm discouraged her.

Babe glanced at her. "After we do the dishes," she said, "your father and I will come out and watch you and the dog."

"Will we, indeed," Albert said. "Mark, eat your lettuce."

"Yes." Babe gave her husband a decisive little nod. "It's only fair."

Albert carved another piece of beef before he answered. "Very well," he said finally.

The light was beginning to fade in the clearing, slanting in through the trees and turning the ground a pale gold.

Sam was nervous, but Cormac went through the commands beautifully. He was enjoying the audience. Out of the corner of her eye Sam could see her father standing with his hands in his pockets, his faded wool plaid shirt hunched up over his bony shoulders.

Cormac completed the final "Heel and sit," and looked up at Sam expectantly. She patted him and they both raced across the grass to the others.

"He really is a sweet dog," Babe said.

Albert laughed. "How do you know he's sweet? You hardly know him."

Babe rubbed the dog's ears. "Do we have to exchange recipes and all that before we can be friends? I like you,

Cormac. You have a sweet face. Albert, look at those nice eyes."

"And those wicked jaws." Albert put his hand on Cormac's head and the dog tensed.

"Easy, boy," Sam said, anxiously. "Daddy, you move too fast."

"It wasn't with their nice gentle eyes that his ancestors exterminated the wolves of Ireland," Albert said to Babe. "The Gaelic slogan says 'Gentle when stroked, fierce when provoked.'" And to Sam he said, "Did you know there's a statue of an Irish wolfhound at Gettysburg?"

"No," Sam said. She wished her father would talk about whether she could keep Cormac.

"Yes, he fought with Meagher's Irish brigade in the Civil War. Meagher of Butte. Columbus brought one with him when he came to America. Oliver Cromwell owned one and Oliver Goldsmith wrote in praise of them."

"Are you making it up?" Babe asked.

"No. I looked up Irish in the library."

"Well, tell Sam whether she can keep him. That's what she wants to know."

"I guess so," Albert said. "If he behaves."

"No, not 'if.' It would be too hard to let her keep him awhile and then have to give him up."

"All right, all right," Albert said. "Keep him. I'll fix it up with Martha."

Sam whooped with joy. She gave her father a quick hug and raced Cormac to the house.

The football field was still dark and there were only a few people in the stadium when Sam got there. She had come early because she was not sure how one behaved at a football game and she didn't want to make a fool of herself. She was wishing now that she had gone to the pep rally at school. She had skipped it so that she could listen to Miss Barracini's new Purcell album. She watched the cheerleaders down on the field. They were shivering in their brief costumes with the purple and orange pompoms.

The field lights went on, and what had been an ordinary place suddenly took on a look of glamour. Sam sat up a little straighter and pulled her leather jacket around her. People were trickling in, a few at a time. The lights in the hot dog stand went on, and she could see the vendor laying a row of hot dogs on the grill, fanning them out like thick fingers. Some boys in sweatshirts and football pants were jogging up and down near the field house. Then the members of the band began to arrive, straggling out onto the field, splendid in purple and gold.

People were arriving in groups and couples, carrying blankets and thermos bottles. The student cheering section was filling up. Sam had avoided sitting there because she didn't know what to do. Now she wished she had.

Then the team burst onto the field like a barrage of buckshot and the students broke into a high, excited yell. Sam found herself on her feet with the others. She didn't know the school yells, but she opened her mouth and yelled anyway.

The visiting team ran onto the field and there was a trickle of applause from the visitors' side of the stadium. Bulky inhuman-looking creatures ran up and down the field. They threw the football, they caught, they feinted, and they pranced with knees high, like circus horses. Sam could hardly believe that these grotesquely lumpy figures were boys she went to school with.

Then with a great clash of sound the band marched onto the field and Sam jumped to her feet with the other spectators. She felt terribly exhilarated and proud. She was not sure why. But somehow the field had been touched with magic. It was heroic and bigger than life. The band wheeled and marched and wheeled again like a fluid carpet of brilliant flowers. She wondered if the Roman spectators had felt like this when they watched the gladiators.

She searched for the French horns. They were not hard to find, but it was almost beyond belief that one player of the horns was her little brother. He looked tremendously tall and erect. At home he always slumped and slouched, but tonight he carried himself with military majesty. Where had he learned such beautiful precision? How had he suddenly become so handsome? And why had he not told her what was happening to him?

Even when the two rows of heroes lined up for the kickoff, and then began to hurl themselves at each other in mysterious fashion, she could not take her eyes off the band. They sat in a colorful phalanx. Mark was at the end of one row, sitting very straight and motionless. She thought that if he should turn his head and look up at her, she would be too shy to speak to him. He was a beautiful stranger with a secret life.

Finally she brought her attention back to the game. She could make no sense of it. At first the screaming crowd, that surged up every few minutes with incomprehensible yells, was exciting, but soon she lost her feeling of unity with them, and began to watch objectively. The players seemed to be in a constant tangle of flailing arms and legs, body smashing against body.

But the band retained its glory. At the half-time she watched enthralled as they paraded and pivoted and and turned, and finally spelled out FHS. One boy, almost hidden by his bass drum, made a fine, smart turn to the left when the band turned right, and one majorette twirled her baton with such abandon that she dropped it, but these were minor flaws in a major display.

When the game was over, Sam stayed in her seat to wait for Mark. Miss Barracini stopped beside her. Her cheeks glowed from the cold air, and her eyes were warm and friendly.

"What are you doing here alone?" she asked. She

was wearing navy-blue flannel slacks and a loose-knit sweater that made her look very young and pretty. Mr. Stone, the math teacher, had a firm grip on her elbow.

Sam gazed at her in open admiration. It seemed to her that she had never seen anyone so beautiful. Then she remembered that she had been asked a question. "I'm waiting for my brother," she said.

"Why aren't you in the student section?" Mr. Stone asked. He was a tall, stiff young man with dark red, crinkly hair and strange red-brown eyes that you couldn't see into. He liked Sam because she did well in algebra.

"I don't know," Sam said. It was a foolish answer.

"Next time sit with the students." He nodded sagely.

Miss Barracini smiled and bent her head down. Her lips brushed Sam's cheek. "You sit where you like," she whispered. And she and Mr. Stone went on down the stadium steps. He stepped with a cautious and heavy tread, and Miss Barracini floated like a cloud. Dazed, Sam put her hand to her cheek. She wanted to run after Miss Barracini and tell her that she loved her very much. But of course she could not possibly do that.

A few minutes later she was aware that someone else stood beside her. It was one of the cheerleaders, Ellen May Aronson, probably the most popular girl in school. In her sophomore year she was already undisputed leader of the most exclusive clique. Sam admired her. Ellen May had smooth, honey-blonde hair that hung to her shoulders, and light blue eyes that looked at the world without surprise. She was built like Jayne Mansfield, and she drove a bright red Thunderbird, registered in her own name.

"Hi," she said to Sam.

"Hi." Sam could not remember that Ellen May had ever even looked at her before.

"How'd you like the game?" she said.

"Fine," Sam said cautiously. It seemed like a safe answer, since they had won.

"That's your brother, isn't it—the tall one with the French horn?" Ellen May stood with one foot on the cement bench, carelessly twirling her baton.

"Yes. Why?"

"Oh, nothing," Ellen May said. She looked at Sam with a quick, sidelong glance. "He's dreamy."

Sam thought she must have misunderstood. Her brother was fun, and he was wise about many things, and as of tonight he was alien and beautiful. But dreamy?

"You-all going to the school dance next Friday?"

"I don't know," Sam said. She had seen the posters but it hadn't occurred to her to go. She didn't know how to dance.

"Why don't you and your brother come, and hang around with our crowd?"

Sam couldn't believe what she was hearing. Ellen May's crowd was the most exclusive group in the school. They never mixed with the others.

"Your crowd?" Sam was afraid she sounded stupid, and Ellen May would withdraw the invitation. "Thank you . . ."

"That's OK." Ellen May waved her baton airily, like a queen acknowledging her subjects. "Don't forget to bring your brother." She looked down at a group of boys who were calling impatiently. "Bye-bye," she said to Sam. "See you." And she skipped down the stadium steps.

Sam was glad when the lights went out and she could sit for a minute looking out over what was once again an ordinary field. So many things had happened since she first walked into the stadium. The strange, wild game, the transformation of her brother, Miss Barracini's warmth, and now the invitation from Ellen May. It was more than she could grasp all at once.

When Mark came for her, she looked at him in astonishment. He wore his old blue jeans and ski jacket, and he looked at her as if nothing at all had happened. "Well, are you coming?" he asked in mild impatience.

She had almost always shared new experiences with Mark; it was part of the pleasure. But tonight she could think of almost nothing to say to him. He too seemed absorbed, and they went home together in unusual silence.

Sam went out to the barn to say good-night to Cormac, and then she came into the house.

"How was the game?" Albert asked. Sam lingered near the living room door, feeling a new need for solitude. "Fine. Only I don't really understand what they were doing."

"It's just a problem in overcoming obstacles to reach a given goal," Albert said.

"That helps a lot," Sam said.

He laughed. "It's a ritual, honey child, complicated beyond belief, as all rituals are, from the bullfight to the church."

"Why do they yell so much?" Sam said. "I never could tell what they were yelling about."

"Part of the rite." Albert leaned his elbow on the mantel, and Sam was sorry she had brought up the question. "Ritual," he went on, "is simply man's feeble attempt to impose order on chaos."

"That's not a nice way to talk about the church," Babe said.

"Daughter, learn from your mother," Albert said, half teasing, half irritated. "She can stop a discussion cold dead in its track just by saying it isn't nice. There's no answer to such a statement."

"How did Mark do?" Babe looked fondly at her son, who lay on his back on the floor, reading a ham radio operator's magazine.

"Fine," Sam said remotely. Then it occurred to her to be nice. "Would you like to go to the next game with me, Mother?"

Babe looked up with such a radiant flash of surprise that Sam was stricken with remorse at her own thoughtlessness. She should have asked her mother to go tonight.

"I'd love to, dear," Babe said.

Sam came and sat on the hearth near her mother.

Mark glanced up. "I don't know if I'll stay in the band."

"Why in the world not?" Babe said. "It's an honor."

"They waste too much time practicing. I have other things to do." He looked at his father for support. "I have to bone up for my conditional license."

"I thought you just got your whatever it is," Albert said.

"Novice. But I can get the provisional as soon as I can do thirteen w.p.m. And I can almost do it now."

"I hope you'll stay in the band," Babe said.

"Why?" Albert said.

"The children . . ." Babe hated to be forced into logical explanations. "They aren't used to group things, and there's pleasure to be had . . ."

"Like what?"

"Like friendship." Babe put down her knitting. "Like learning to understand people and exchanging ideas. Like just enjoying people."

Albert looked at her thoughtfully for a moment. Then he turned to Sam. "If you really want to know how a football game works, this is it: there are two teams of eleven players. They line up like this . . ." He went on explaining the game. Babe sighed and went back to her knitting.

Sam half listened as her father moved matches around on the coffee table to illustrate various plays. Her mind was on Mark.

"We're invited to go to the school dance with Ellen May's crowd," she said finally.

Babe looked pleased. "How nice."

Mark looked up suspiciously. "Who's we?"

"You and me. It's going to be a swinging dance."

"It will swing without me," Mark said.

"Oh, Mark," his mother said.

"Mother," he said, "Ellen May Aronson has the I.Q. of a backward amoeba."

"She's the most popular girl in school," Sam said.

"Big deal."

"It wouldn't hurt you to take your sister," Babe said.

He looked pained. "Mother, that is the snobbiest bunch in school."

"Then why did they ask us?" Sam said.

He looked at her, frowning. "Sam, they're phonies. Thatcher and Ellen May—the Golden Girl and the Golden Boy—which means they run their crowd like feudal tyrants. They've got a regular power structure.

One of them gives the word to one of their aides—do this, do that—and it's done."

"It sounds like the Mafia," Albert said.

"It isn't so different. Last spring the school decided to close the snack shop because the cafeteria was losing money. Thatcher and Aronson put out the word: boycott the cafeteria. In one whole week not more than two dozen kids went into the cafeteria. The school reopened the snack shop."

"Oh, Mark, you must be exaggerating," Babe said.

He shook his head. "Mom, you just don't know. Even Mr. Stone will tell you."

"But everybody belongs to groups," Sam said. "*I* ate at the cafeteria."

"Sure, so did I," Mark said. "And how many others?"

"Well," Sam said reluctantly, "there weren't many, but the cafeteria isn't very much fun."

Mark shrugged. "Sam hasn't got the concept of The Group yet. She thinks people are just people."

"Well, they are," she said.

"Some are," he said. "There's Eric Benson and George Weaver and a few of the girls—and a few more, not many. You learn to spot them."

"What about the people who can't get into the group?" Albert asked.

"They form their own group. I've made a study of this. There are at least seven groups in that high school, and they go down the scale in importance."

"And where do you fit into this fascinating hierarchy?" Albert asked.

Mark grinned. "You might say I'm a serf who looks on and thinks."

Sam felt depressed. She didn't know whether Mark

was right or not. Or whether it made any difference. She still wanted to go to the dance.

"How do you get to be a Golden Girl or a Golden Boy?" Albert asked.

"Ellen May owns her own T-Bird. She always has plenty of dough. And she's loud. Terry Thatcher is the big athlete, and terribly, terribly suave." Mark struck a pose. "May I light your cigarillo, madam?"

Albert laughed. Babe sighed and said, "Why does a simple invitation have to get so complicated?"

Albert swept the match football players into his hand. "I told you. Send them off the island and life gets complex."

"Nevertheless," Sam said, "I cannot grow up like Rima the Bird Girl. I want to go to the dance. It's the first time I've been invited to anything by anybody. I want to find out what goes on in the world."

"You'll find out," Mark said. "Guaranteed."

"The only thing is," Sam said, "I can't dance."

"I'll teach you," Babe said.

"Can you do the latest dances?" Mark asked her.

"Oh, they can't be so different," Babe said.

Sam felt like crying. "I'm going anyway. I'm sick of being an outsider. After all, I'm *in* that school; I might as well act like it."

"Mr. Stone says . . ." Mark began.

"I don't care what Mr. Stone says."

Babe put up her knitting and got up briskly. "What we all need is food," she said. "Nobody ate enough dinner. Come on and I'll make sandwiches. We can use that good cheddar . . ."

Albert was looking at the matches as if they meant something. "All right," he said.

Although Mark steadfastly refused to go to the school dance, Sam went anyway. Her father drove her up to the gym entrance. Cars were parked all up and down the wide street and in the school parking lot.

"When I was a kid," Albert said, "we walked."

Sam was afraid to get out. In the back of the pickup, Cormac scratched impatiently on the metal floor. He was along only because he got out and came running up at the last minute—too late to take him back to the barn. Albert leaned out and told him to sit.

"Go ahead," Albert said to Sam. "I don't want Cormac leaping out and running off." He reached past her and opened the door. "I'll pick you up at eleven-thirty, right here."

She got out because she couldn't think of any way to put it off. In despair she watched the pickup drive away. She had never felt so alone in her life. The car diminished to a vague shape, the small eye of the taillight twinkling.

As the car turned the corner, she saw the pale shape of Cormac. Then they were gone.

Couples and groups of boys and girls were arriving and parking their cars and walking up to the gym door, talking and laughing excitedly. Every time the door was opened the sound of dance music washed over the street. It was loud music with a strong beat. Sam wondered if she could possibly dance to it in the way her mother had taught her.

She moved off into the shadows of a group of willow trees, and hesitantly tried a few steps of what her mother called the fox-trot. She couldn't seem to keep time.

She pulled back further into the darkness when she saw Ellen May's Thunderbird drive up. Ellen May got out, and another girl and two boys swarmed out, laughing and yelling at each other. She saw them clearly when the pool of light from the gym fell on them in the doorway. The boys wore suits and ties, and they looked almost as strange as the football boys had looked in their uniforms. The girls looked like illustrations from a fashion magazine.

Ellen May and her friends disappeared into the warm tumult of the gym. Sam shivered. What am I doing here? she said under her breath. But it was too late to flee. Her father wouldn't come for three hours, and there was nowhere else to go. She thought for a moment of the town library, but it was a long walk and it closed at nine. There was nothing to do but go in.

She waited until no one was in sight. Then she walked quickly across the frozen grass to the gym door. She pulled open the heavy door before she could allow herself time to panic.

The lights, the pound of the music, the heat, and

the density of many people crowding the gym, which didn't look like the gym at all, made Sam stand still for a moment, dazed. Japanese lanterns were strung. At the far end, on a small raised platform, a combo made up of high school boys beat out the sound. The floor was crowded with swinging, swaying dancers. Most of them danced apart from each other. No one was doing a fox-trot.

She looked at the girls. Some of them looked frilly and some looked sleek, and some had their faces made up like masks.

No one, absolutely no one, was wearing a simple dark-blue wool. For a moment she felt angry at her mother. Fox-trots and blue wools! But how could her mother know? She never got off the stupid island.

Three girls whom she knew slightly brushed past her. One looked back and said, "Hi," and then the others turned and said, "Hi, Sam."

"Hi," Sam said. She had never thought much of them, but now they seemed like bosom friends. She gave them her friendliest smile. Be my friends, she wanted to say; talk to me. Please!

They turned back to her. "Who did you come with?" asked Mary Beth, the one who had spoken first. The three of them clung together with the strained look of dateless girls.

"I just came by myself," Sam said. "My brother was going to come with me but he—he couldn't make it."

"Brothers," said Anna, the plump Swedish girl.

Sam couldn't let Mark be included in such a category. "He just doesn't like dances," she said.

"They never do," said Anna.

"You want to stick with us?" Mary Beth asked. She was a tall, stringy girl, near-sighted and good in math.

Sam felt torn. Here was a kind of security. But across the room was Ellen May, surrounded by glamor. And she had asked Sam. "Ellen May Aronson asked me to join her bunch," Sam said. "Thank you just the same, though."

There was an unmistakable flicker of hostility in their exchanged glance. "Ellen May," Anna said. "Well."

Hester raised up on her toes, mincing. "The Golden Girl." They began to move away.

"Thank you anyway," Sam said. "Please don't think —I mean, she did ask me."

"That's OK," Anna said. They pushed off along the crowded edge of the floor.

The combo, in funny hats, tore into a chorus. Feeling vaguely depressed, Sam watched the girls make their way toward the long table where punch bowls and plates of cookies were arranged on a crepe paper table cloth. Perhaps she should have gone with them. And yet why go to a dance at all if you're going to slink along the wall with other girls? She looked around for Ellen May, and after a moment she saw her dancing with Terry Thatcher.

A couple came toward her, dancing together, unlike the other dancers. As they came closer, weaving their way through the crowd, Sam saw that it was Miss Barracini and Mr. Stone.

They saw her and steered their course toward her. Sam had never seen a schooner, but she imagined it would look like Mr. Stone, square and powerful. When they reached her, Miss Barracini broke away from Mr. Stone and fanned herself with a little lace-edged handkerchief. "Sam," she said, "how nice to see you. You look like a cool violet in this wild hothouse." She smiled at

Mr. Stone. "How's that for a metaphor?"

"Very good." He beamed at her with admiration.

Miss Barracini said, "Whom are you with, Sam?"

Sam realized that it was essential to be with someone. "Ellen May Aronson asked me to join her crowd," she said. "But I haven't caught up with her yet."

Miss Barracini raised her eyebrows. "Ellen May."

"Well, she asked me at the football game, Mark and me."

"Oh." Miss Barracini looked as if that explained something. She glanced past Sam. "Is Mark here?"

"He wouldn't come."

Mr. Stone chuckled. "Smart boy." He mopped his brow.

"If you get hung up or anything," Miss Barracini said, "come and talk to us."

"Thank you very much," Sam said. It was nice of Miss Barracini. But you didn't come to a school dance to talk to teachers. Not even Miss Barracini.

The music stopped. It was now or never. "Excuse me," Sam said. She dove into the crowd and headed for the corner where Ellen May was. Sam was tall enough that she could see over many heads, and she kept Ellen May's scarlet skirt in view.

There was a crowd around Ellen May, as usual. And Terry Thatcher was there, too, of course. Sam looked at the group closely as she came up to them. Did they really have aides and all that, the way Mark said? He might have imagined it. The thing that interested Sam most at that moment was that they seemed to be having such a good time. There was a lot of laughter.

Ellen May caught her eye. "Come on in," she said.

The phalanx parted and Sam stepped in. She glanced

shyly at Terry Thatcher. She had thought for a long time that he was the handsomest boy in school.

When she was actually there, Sam felt suddenly shy. She tried to tell herself it was crazy; they were only kids, like any other kids. But this was not true. They *were* being treated like some kind of royalty, just the way Mark said. Sam felt like running away. But it was too late.

"Hey, hi," Ellen May said. "Hey, gang, this is Sam something."

Sam tried to say her last name but it was lost in the buzz of polite response to Ellen May's introduction. Kids she knew perfectly well were saying hello as if they had never met her before.

"And not a minute too soon," said Terry Thatcher. "Where have you been all my life, old Uncle Sam?"

Everyone laughed except Ellen May. "Where is your brother?" she said.

"Seriously, where have you been?" said Terry.

"I'm in your English class," she said shyly.

"Who isn't?" He made a face. "I'm taking it for the second time."

"Where is your brother?" Ellen said, more loudly.

"He couldn't come," Sam said. "Something came up . . . ." She broke off. She was not good at lying. And the light of welcome had gone out of Ellen May's face.

"Oh, crap. Terry, get me some punch." She turned her back on Sam.

Terry snapped his fingers. "Henny Penny, get milady some punch." And a thin boy with wavy blond hair trotted off obediently.

"I said *you*." Ellen May's eyes blazed angrily.

"Sorry," Terry said. "I'm dancing this one with Debby." He wheeled his way out of the group as the music started.

Sam suddenly felt very much alone. I'd better go home, she thought. I'd better get out of here. But before she could move, Anna and Hester and Mary Beth swept by her.

"Hey, how's the view from the top?" Anna said loudly.

They all giggled and kept on going.

Sam started for the door, trying to dodge the chattering groups. She avoided looking toward the chaperones' corner.

A boy detached himself from a folding chair near the wall and came over to her. "Hi," he said.

"Hi," Sam said. She moved to go by him. She just wanted to get outside where she could breathe. And where no one would look at her as if she were a freak.

But the boy moved along with her. "I'm in your Chem class," he said.

She looked at him. It was a junior, named Eric something. He had a round freckled face and his hair was pale red. For some reason he seemed glad to see her.

"I know," she said. "How are you."

He looked encouraged. "Isn't this a lousy bash?"

"I don't really know," Sam said. "I've never been to one before."

"Never been to a dance? You're kidding!"

"It's not the sort of thing you kid about," Sam said sharply.

"Listen," he said, "would you like some punch?"

She started to say no but over his shoulder she saw the three girls watching. "Yes," she said. "Thank you."

"OK, stick close and we'll lick this mob." He led her toward the refreshment table. He was not very tall, and he had to keep ducking elbows and changing course.

At last he managed to get two Lily cups of punch. "Follow me," he said. And he pushed on ahead of her to an areaway that connected the gym and the locker rooms. He made a place for her to sit on top of a stack of tumbling mats. It was cool and relatively quiet. "There," he said. He gave her a cup.

"This is nice. Thank you." He was kind.

"Say, were you kidding, about never having been to a party? I mean, I can't believe it."

"Well, it's true," she said.

He shook his head. "Boy, are you lucky!"

"Lucky! Why?"

"Listen, I've been going to parties practically since I was born. And I've hated every one of them."

"Then why do you go?"

He shrugged. "My mother says go, I go. I am mother-dominated, if you want to know the truth."

"Why does she want you to go to parties?"

"She says it will develop my social graces. I think, personally, it's a losing fight."

"I think you have very nice social graces," Sam said. She meant it.

"You women hang together." He drank off the cup of punch. "Look at that. I'm a glutton, among other things."

"Are there lots of parties?" Sam asked.

"Thousands. Tonight I not only had to go to this thing, but I had to go to the party Ellen May Aronson gave beforehand. I don't usually travel with that crowd, but they were short of boys. My greatest contribution to society is as an extra boy."

"Wasn't it any fun?"

"It was fiendish."

"I shouldn't even be here," Sam said. "The only dance I know is the fox-trot."

"You want to learn those dances?"

"I never could."

"Sure you can. Let a master teach you." He grinned at her and began beating out the rhythm with his foot. Then he started a slow swaying of the hips. "This is one of them. It's kind of out now but some kids still do it."

"That's really strange," Sam said.

"And this one." He showed her. "See, they aren't so different."

"I didn't even know the fox-trot till a few days ago," Sam said.

"This is easier. Here, try it." He took her hand. "It's stupid, but it's kind of fun actually."

Hesitantly Sam tried.

"Not bad. Only see, more sideways. In a way it's almost like the rhumba."

"I don't know the rhumba," Sam said. "Not even by sight."

He laughed. "Well, it's not all that tragic. Hey, you're getting it."

"I am?" It began to seem easier.

"Want to try it on the dance floor?"

"Oh, no!" She could imagine everyone laughing at her.

"Well, would you like to go for a soda? I don't have a car but Manuel's is only three blocks."

"It would be nice," Sam said. "But my father is coming for me. Eleven thirty."

"I'll get you back long before that. If you're worrying, I can assure you that I'm nauseatingly dependable."

Sam laughed. "I wasn't worrying." She was about to say yes. He was very nice and funny.

But before she could answer, Terry Thatcher saw them and came loping down the areaway. "Uncle Sam!" he said. "I've been looking everywhere for you."

"Me?" Sam thought it must be mistaken identity.

"You." His dark eyes sparkled. "You and I are going to dance, O Sam."

Panic choked Sam "I can't. I don't dance."

"Then I'll teach you." He grabbed her hand. He was very tall.

"She happens to be with me at the moment," Eric said.

Terry laughed. He gave Eric a playful shove with the flat of his hand.

Sam saw Eric lose his balance and stumble backward. She saw the flush of humiliation on his neck and face. "I'm with Eric," she said.

Terry took her hand. "Old Eric will understand." He pulled her toward the dance floor.

Sam tried to look back, but Terry guided her onto the dance floor and into the crowd. He held her hands and started to dance.

For a moment Sam was too frightened to move. Then, with Terry nodding encouragement, she began to dance as Eric had shown her. Stiffly at first, and then as the beat of the combo pounded out insistently, she began to relax and move with it. Terry smiled approvingly and let go of her hands. As long as she didn't think about what she was doing, it came out all right. It began to be fun. The constant rhythm, the gay bobbing Japanese lanterns overhead, the colorful moving mass of people swirling all around her—it was exciting, almost intoxicating, like the carnival only better. When the music stopped, she felt cheated.

"You were great!" He danced with her for a long time. Finally he steered her off the floor.

Ellen May and her partner pushed past them, and Ellen gave her a cold, hard look, but Sam forgot it almost as soon as it had happened.

They joined Debby Frye, the senior class president, and a big beefy boy named Axel Hansen, who was captain of the football team. Sam had always admired Debby, but she had never thought of speaking to her.

"Meet Sam," said Terry. He put his arm around her shoulders as if she were his discovery. "She's terrific."

Debby smiled and said, "Hi, Sam."

"Hey, good buddies, let's get some of that ptomaine-type punch and go out on the terrace," Terry said.

As they stopped at the refreshment table, Sam caught Miss Barracini's eye. Miss Barracini nodded and smiled. So being in the group wasn't at all what Mark had said. It was wonderful. She felt like a new Sam. She had danced all evening with the Golden Boy himself, and she hadn't even tried to make it happen.

At the door Eric stopped her. "Here's your coat," he said. He gave it to her and left before she could even say thank you. He hadn't looked mad. He hadn't looked anything at all, except sort of cool and far-off.

"Now, there's a little gentleman," Terry said. He put the coat over her shoulders.

"I ought to speak to him . . ." Sam started after Eric. She couldn't just let him go like that, when he had been so nice.

Terry caught her arm. "He's gone. Come on."

It was cold and clear outside. Terry spread out his handkerchief on the cement retaining wall and lifted Sam onto it. He handed her a cup of punch, with an exaggerated bow. "Here's to Uncle Sam. Long may she wave."

Sam smiled, and ate cookies, and listened while the other three criticized the dance, the combo, the refreshments, the school. The boys were the most critical. Debby mostly listened and laughed and made a remark now and then.

Overhead, the sky was dazzling with stars, and a thin wedge of moon rested on the tops of the jack pines. The pounding of the combo reached them as if from far away. It was nicest of all, Sam thought, to be part of everything and still just a little outside it, like this.

The boys were analyzing a practice basketball game. Terry was saying he had had an off night. Sam hoped they wouldn't discover that she had never seen a basketball game. Sometime she would go.

"Hey, you're a quiet chick," Axel said to her suddenly. "Don't you ever talk?"

"With you two around, who can talk?" Debby said. She smiled at Sam. Debby was nice. Axel wasn't all that nice, Sam decided. He had something heavy and harsh about him. Maybe it was his squareness. Everything about him looked square—shoulders, hands, even his head.

A boy came out from the hall. "Hey, Terry. Ellen May says you got this dance with her."

"Tell her I'm busy." Terry grinned.

The boy shrugged and went away.

"Shouldn't you go?" Sam asked.

"Let her highness sweat it out," Terry said. "It'll do her good."

"Oh, Terry," Debby said.

"Nobody owns me." For a second, Terry glowered. Then he cheered up and said, "Hey, more punch all around?"

"Good idea," Debby said.

"Axel, old buddy, you do the honors. I'll protect the ladies," Terry said.

Ungraciously Axel slid off the wall. "You would." He went into the hall.

The band played a flourish and called intermission. Couples and groups began to wander out onto the terrace. Sam saw Miss Barracini and Mr. Stone come out. People stopped to chat with Terry and Debby. Some of them smiled at Sam, some said, "Hi." One girl said she had a pretty dress. Sam couldn't believe it, but she was grateful. She felt as if she were floating in a glow of reflected glory. She wondered if Guinevere's ladies-in-waiting felt this way.

Axel came back, balancing four cups.

"Well done, O Knight," said Terry, and they all laughed as if he had said something terribly witty.

"Ellen May is fit to be tied," Axel said.

"So tie her." Terry laughed. He looked pleased.

"I mean it," Axel said. "She's really tensed up."

"She'll get over it." He lifted his cup. "To us, to us, to beautiful, swinging us." His dark eyes smiled warmly at Sam. She felt a little dizzy.

She saw Terry's glance go past her and his expression change. She looked over her shoulder and saw Ellen May and a group of people. Ellen May swept by without a glance at Terry. He chuckled.

And then without warning a huge, gray form soared over the retaining wall. Before she fully saw him, Sam knew it was Cormac. He landed at her feet. Cups of punch flew through the air. Girls screamed. And Terry was knocked flat on his back. He lay still. There was a long moment of stunned silence.

"Terry!" It was Debby's voice, high and strained. She bent over Terry. Sticky red punch stained the front of her dress. Miss Barracini and Mr. Stone pushed through the crowd. Then Terry opened his eyes, stared blankly upward for a moment, and began to struggle to his feet.

Mr. Stone reached him. "All right, Thatcher?"

Furiously Terry pushed away Mr. Stone's helping hands. "How do I know?" His voice sounded thick. He looked at Cormac, who sat at Sam's feet panting happily. "Is that monster yours?" His eyes were glassy with anger.

"I'm so sorry," Sam said faintly. "I'm so sorry. Are you hurt?"

"You may just have ruined the whole basketball season, that's all," he said. He touched his elbows gingerly. "I could sue you."

"Oh, come on, Thatcher," Miss Barracini said. "You haven't hurt anything but your dignity."

Ellen May began to laugh. At first the others looked at her uneasily, but then they began to join in, and in a minute there was a roar of laughter. Terry turned white with humiliation and rage.

Mr. Stone waved his arms for attention. "All right, all right," he said, "break it up. Everybody inside. There's no harm done."

"Listen!" Terry said. "I may have a concussion!"

"I doubt it," said Mr. Stone calmly.

Sam was too stricken to speak. Miss Barracini touched her arm. "He's all right, Sam. And that's a beautiful dog."

Terry limped off, toward the street. The others except for Debby and Axel were herded back into the auditorium by a firm Mr. Stone. Sam looked at Cormac. He cocked his head innocently.

"How could you!" she said.

"Don't worry about it," Miss Barracini said. "Thatcher needed a comedown."

Sam couldn't explain to her that a whole golden world had vanished. She felt like Cinderella. Numbly she watched Miss Barracini patting Cormac's head. "You ought to show him, Sam," she said. "He's really magnificent."

Debby nodded her head. "He looks as good as any Irish I've seen when I've taken my mutt to dog shows."

Sam smiled weakly, but didn't reply. She heard the roar of the pickup, and in a moment her father came up the walk, his faded khakis flapping around his thin legs. He looked different to her, as if he had changed or as if she were seeing him for the first time. "Sam?" he called out. Then he saw her. "Is Cormac here?" He came onto the terrace and looked at Cormac, who bounded over to greet him. "You big stupid oaf," Albert said to Cormac. He looked at Miss Barracini. "I'm Sam's father. I hope the dog didn't do any harm. He chewed through his leash while I was having a cup of coffee . . ."

"No harm done," Miss Barracini said. "He was just a little startling for a minute."

"I know," Albert said. "He's so bloody big."

No harm done, Sam thought bitterly.

105

"Good night," she said politely to Miss Barracini, in a faraway voice. And she went down the walk to the pickup.

On the ride back to the boat her father made a few attempts to talk to her but she sat huddled in the corner, the tears silently streaking her face. I am a fool, she kept saying over and over in her mind. I am a fool, a fool, a fool. When she looked back at it now, it was all terribly clear. Terry hadn't really been so attracted to her. He was just trying to make Ellen May mad. They had had a fight or something.

When they got home, she ran upstairs to her room, not waiting to talk to her mother, who had sat up to hear about the dance. Before she got into bed, she got out her journal and wrote, "Know thyself," and underlined it four times.

She could hear them talking downstairs. Her father was telling her mother what happened. "Some kid got knocked down," he said.

"Oh, no!" her mother said. "I did so want it to be a lovely evening for her."

"Well, if you insist on letting the kids mess around in town, that's what can happen," Albert said.

Babe sounded annoyed. "Going to a school dance isn't exactly messing around."

"In this case it was fairly messy. That kid could sue me."

"Albert, you cannot keep them locked up on this island."

Now he was sounding angry. "Why can't I?"

"Because it isn't normal."

"Define 'normal,' would you please?"

Sam couldn't stand it. She flew out of bed and down

the stairs in her bare feet. She was incandescent with rage. Her parents looked up, startled. "Just stop fighting about me," she said. "Stop it, right now."

Neither of them spoke.

"I am sick of this. I cannot spend my life on the island like some little badger . . ." She saw the hurt look on her father's face. She turned to her mother. "And that world across the river is not the great big Valentine you think it is. People tell lies—they don't mean what they say . . . and . . ." She took a quivering breath. "I will decide what is going to happen to my life. I. Me. Nobody else. Now I'm going to sleep in the barn for the rest of the night."

"Put on some shoes," Babe called, but Sam ignored her, and ran fast on the cold ground in her bare feet.

She pushed Cormac away, and wrapped a horse blanket around herself. He stretched out next to her and finally she looked at him. "It's been a night, all right. And you were a great, great help." Cormac looked at her and blinked sleepily. "I made a fool of myself," she said. "I thought it was me Ellen May was inviting, but it was only Mark. And I was very rude to Eric what's-his-name. And now I've been yelling at my parents. I can't feel anything any more. I'm played out." She leaned her head against the rough boards of the stall. "Somewhere there *must* be a book of rules or something that tells you how to act. How to know." She looked at Cormac. "And you've got to learn some obedience, or Dad will get rid of you."

Frightened, she put her arms around his neck, and the two of them fell asleep.

Sam sat upright. Her first waking thought was of the dance. She tried to put it out of her mind, but the scene lit up in her mind as if someone had flipped a switch. She groaned and leaned her head on her arms. Cormac woke up and pushed against her arm.

"How will I face them at school on Monday?" she said. "They'll all be laughing."

A shaft of light fell across her knees. Her mother was coming down the path of sunlight that the opened door let in on the barn floor. How sure she looks, Sam thought. Things must have been so much simpler when she was young.

Her mother looked down at her. She looked serious but not angry or hurt. She was wearing a freshly-laundered light-blue shirt and clean blue jeans that fitted neatly around her small hips. Her hair was still damp around her face from the shower and her face glowed. "Good morning," she said.

"Hi," Sam said cautiously.

"Time for breakfast."

Sam closed her eyes. "I don't think I want any."

"Oh, I think you will," her mother said. She looked at Sam a moment. "Things aren't all that bad."

"That's what you think," Sam said miserably.

"Things are never as bad as you think. Believe me, never. People aren't as concerned with you as you think they are."

"I don't feel well," Sam said.

"You'll feel better after breakfast." Babe walked back along the sunny path of the floor on her silent, sneakered feet. She paused to pat the milk cow. "A hot shower and some breakfast will do wonders." She went out.

"The world collapses and your mother recommends a hot shower," Sam said. She got to her feet. She felt stiff. She wondered how Terry felt.

At the house she showered and dressed. She didn't like to admit it, but she did feel a little better. Just a little.

Mark was waiting impatiently. He had promised to help her work with Cormac. "Hurry up," he said.

Sam wondered if he had heard about last night.

"You don't have to be in such a rush," his mother told him. "There's time. Sam, eat some toast."

Sam shook her head.

"Mark, Sam will be along in a minute."

When he was gone, Babe gave Sam some toast, lightly buttered and crunchy, the way she liked it.

"I'm sorry I was such a brat last night," Sam said. She bit into the toast.

"I know you are," Babe said. "You were partly right. Not in losing your temper, but in what you said. You *are* growing up, and we're going to have to let you make your own decisions."

Sam broke the toast in half with great concentration. "It wasn't so much a question of decisions."

"But decisions are always involved," Babe said. "To go to the dance or not to go. To pay attention to one person or another. There are always decisions." She waited. "I'm sorry Cormac spoiled things."

"I don't suppose he really did," Sam said. "He just kind of brought things to light."

Babe got some aluminum foil and put another piece of toast in it and carefully wrapped it. "Eat it outside."

"Thanks," Sam said. At the door she turned back. "Thanks, Mom."

Babe smiled. And Sam ran down the path holding her package of toast in her hands.

MONDAY AT SCHOOL WAS NOT SO VERY DIFFERENT AFTER all. Most of the people who usually paid no attention to her still paid no attention, or at most gave her only a curious glance. But being ignored was more painful now because for a little while at the dance she had not been ignored.

When Terry turned his head away as he passed her in the hall, she wished for the days when he hadn't spoken to her because he simply hadn't noticed her. Now he hated her. Ellen May looked at her as if she were a new and peculiar species. Mary Beth and Anna and Hester were almost alarmingly friendly. Debby was not in school.

She stopped outside the chemistry lab to brace herself for the encounter with Eric. But when she went in, he simply looked up from his Bunsen burner and nodded, as he always did. She had been nervously rehearsing apologies, but his casual manner made apology impossible.

That he would not allow her a repentance scene was a thought that had not occurred to her. Somehow it was worse than any of the possible scenes that she had imagined. Once or twice she decided to speak to him anyway but each time she lost her nerve. She was so abstracted that the teacher had to speak to her sharply. And just before the end of class she dropped a test tube that she was washing out. It made a tinkling sound, like a Christmas ornament breaking. She knelt to pick up the glass.

"Watch it," Eric said. "You've cut your hand."

She looked at the tiny smear of blood. Eric got a dustpan and brush. Gazing up at him Sam said, "Eric . . ." She meant to say, "Eric, forgive me," but the class bell whirred like an angry locust, and the scrape and clatter of departing students were all around her.

"Move," Eric said, "so I can sweep it up." He spoke with the same impersonal impatience that Mark often used. She got to her feet.

"Thanks, Eric," she said. "Thanks."

But he didn't look up.

When she got home from school, Sam got Cormac and her horse. She rode hard across the meadow and into the woods. It was a cold, brilliantly sunny afternoon, and wind tore at her, tangling her hair and whipping color into her cheeks. She reined in the horse, at last, when Cormac flopped down on the ground, panting.

She slid off the horse. "Poor old Cormac. We wore you out." Tired herself, she stretched out on a pile of pine branches. Cormac crawled toward her. He let his hind legs stretch out behind him and he wriggled on his front legs until his head was resting on her knee.

She laughed. "You look three miles long when you do

that." She tilted her head back to see the blue patches of sky through the trees. An aspen leaf, like a thin copper coin, spiraled down and brushed against her face. The world was not so grim as she had thought. Mark was right—out here was the safe and lovely world, away from people. Her horse nuzzled her neck and whinnied.

"All right, old man." She rubbed his nose. "I love you, too. I love you and Cormac and Miss Barracini."

She rolled over and stretched. It was not her fault if Eric didn't let her apologize, and she didn't really care whether Ellen May and Terry ever spoke to her again. They only said mean things when they did speak.

She closed her eyes and sighed. As soon as she could manage it without stirring up a family feud, she would stop school altogether. A person could get knowledge from books. She would stay on the island all her life, reading and playing records and living a very ascetic life. Like Thoreau. "Only that day dawns to which we are awake." It would be a lovely life. She would observe everything in nature, and think a great deal, and maybe write. She yawned and turned over on her side.

When she woke, she was shivering. The sun had slipped down the western sky and she was in shadow. She whistled for her horse, and when he came, she started back. Once she got into the clearing, there was sunshine again. She walked the horse slowly, and waited once or twice while Cormac galloped off to pursue an interesting scent.

Finally he tore off into the underbrush and failed to come back when she called him. She whistled and called again. No Cormac. She slid off the gelding, looped the reins around a fire-blackened stump, and set out to find him. It was easy to follow the trail he made through the brush. She was calling impatiently now. She was getting cold and hungry.

At last she heard his deep bark. She called again and he barked again, but he didn't come. There was something different in his bark, urgent. She tried to run toward him but the branches and underbrush caught at her and made her stumble. The ground sloped upward and there were dense patches of juniper that pricked her ankles. She knew every foot of the island but now, in her anxiety, the terrain seemed strange and hostile.

Then she saw Cormac. In her relief, she spoke his name sharply. He looked at her over his shoulder. His yellow eyes were intent and his hackles bristled. He was growling deep in his throat, a low continuous rumble. As Sam came up to him, he moved and blocked her way so that an abrupt rise in the hill was cut off. All at once she remembered. There was a cave there. She and Mark had explored it once. A few years ago they had come upon a wolf cub, rolling on its back in the sun like a puppy. They had been tempted to play with it, but they knew better.

From the looks of Cormac the cave was occupied now, and it was not the time of year for cubs. "Come on," she said, "before you get into trouble." She put her hand on his collar, but he pulled away from her and went closer to the cave. It went through her mind that he was almost through with being a puppy. It made her feel sad. "Cormac, come," she said. "Not today." If Cormac was going to take on a wolf, she wanted to have a gun in her hand, just in case. There might be more than one wolf in there.

She thought of the wolf she had seen in the rim of

firelight on the night that they searched for Uncle Everett. He had been beautiful. She wished that Cormac and the wolf, so much alike in many ways, didn't have to try to destroy each other.

She spoke to the dog again and he turned his head reluctantly, torn between instinct and training. Suddenly there was a savage growling from just inside the cave. Cormac danced sideways and then leaped for the mouth of the cave, but Sam grabbed him around the middle. It took all her strength but she managed to pull him back. She didn't breathe easily until they had crashed their way back to the meadow. She looped her lariat through his collar and rode her horse at a fast trot toward home.

It was almost dark when she got home. The wind had come up and the sky was the deep strong blue of winter twilight. One of the planets shone steadily close to the horizon. Venus?

She stabled and fed her horse and then she and Cormac went and sat beside the pool in the gathering dark. She hated to go into the house.

She leaned back to toss the hair out of her eyes, and felt the prickle of the kinnikinnick bush under her hand. Today I sat in the dark beside an empty pool and felt the sharpness of kinnikinnick on my hand, she thought; and I may be the only person in the world to whom this happened at that moment.

She knew she ought to go in. It was dinner time and her mother would begin to worry. But still she lingered a few minutes more. Just above a pointed fir tree the new moon hung like a scimitar of smoke. But a scimitar of smoke would be an impossibility, she told herself. A wisp of smoke then, shaped like a scimitar. For all she knew, the moon might really be made of smoke.

She heard Mark come tearing up the path from the river and go into the house with the speed of the late-to-dinner. The kitchen door slammed behind him and then she heard him yell with surprise. Curious, Sam got up and went to the house. "Stay," she told Cormac on the back porch. She went inside.

She found Mark and her parents in the living room. There were boxes and wrapping paper all over the floor, and strange-looking pieces of electronic equipment. Mark was unpacking. He was on his knees, like a monk before an altar.

"What is it?" Sam asked.

Her father said, "It seems to be the makings of a short-wave set if your brother can put the right things together. And I have no doubt he can."

"Sure," Mark said. "The instructions are right here." He removed what looked like a regular radio. "It's a Hallicrafters SX-140," he said reverently.

"Where did you get it?" Sam said.

"Uncle Ev. Boy, wait till Mr. Stone sees this!"

Sam looked quickly at her mother. "Where is he?"

"In Vegas," Albert said. "Just as I told you."

"Not in Paris?" Sam felt bitterly betrayed. All along, she had not believed in her father's cynicism; she had been sure that Uncle Ev really meant to go to Paris. "Maybe he just stopped off there first . . ." But even without her father's withering glance, she knew she was being silly. Uncle Ev had made it all up about Paris. He hadn't really trusted her at all.

"Your mother also has a gift from the great Santa Claus," Albert said.

There was a box on the table. Babe touched it with

the tips of her fingers for a second, as if she were imagining the shop it came from. She opened it and shook out a mink stole.

"It's beautiful," Sam said. She was glad her mother had it. At least they had to admit that Uncle Ev was generous.

"Why not?" Albert said. "A number of healthy, god-fearing mink gave their all for it. Everett does have a passion for dead animals."

Babe put it down quickly. "Why do you have to be so nasty? Everybody wears furs."

Albert shrugged. "So wear it in good health, as they say."

"I'll do that." Babe's voice was tight. "I'll wear it when I feed the chickens, or call in the cows, or any of those other glamorous things I do." She left the room.

Albert half rose as if to follow her but changed his mind. Sam picked up the stole and put it around her.

"It's so soft," she said.

"It looks great with your jeans." Albert looked tired all of a sudden. He watched Sam put the fur back in its box. "I wonder why women have such an instinctive yen for furs and jewels."

"Maybe you could take Mother to a concert in Missoula this winter," Sam said. "And she could wear it."

He looked at her thoughtfully. "Maybe I could, at that."

"Did Aunt Martha get a present?"

"Oh, yes. She called. She got some junk jewelry and a thousand dollar check."

"How do you know it's junk?" Mark said. "You haven't seen it."

"I know Everett. He's a junk jewelry man."

"Well, he knows how to pick out a shortwave," Mark said. He looked at his father impishly. "Hey, Dad, we've all got presents but you."

"Oh, I have not been forgotten," Albert said. "My present is Aunt Martha."

They looked at him in dismay. "What do you mean?" Sam said.

"She's arriving Saturday night."

"Oh, no!" Mark looked stricken.

"Oh, yes. While Everett enjoys the Elysian fields, we shall enjoy Martha. Just temporarily, of course," he said, "while she waits for Everett to send for her to share the glorious life."

"Dad," Sam said, "what is Uncle Everett really doing?"

"Gambling his fool head off, I presume. I hope your mother doesn't land in the clink as a receiver of hot mink."

"Do you mean he won it in a poker game or something?" Mark asked. "The radio, too?" He looked alarmed.

"Oh, I don't suppose so," Albert said wearily. "I imagine he hit it big one night and decided to shower presents on everybody. The big wheeler and dealer. You know Everett." He got up. "Where did your mother go?"

"Upstairs," Sam said.

After he had left the room, Sam said, "Mother was about to cry."

"Why?" Mark turned the packing box upside down to make sure he hadn't overlooked anything.

"I guess because she worries about Uncle Ev, and she never gets to go anywhere. I feel like crying myself.

I thought for sure he was going to Paris." She opened the box and touched the mink again. It opened up visions of worlds that just now in the forest she thought she had foresworn.

"I don't know why everybody is so bound and determined to go somewhere," Mark said. "There's nothing but a bunch of dumb people."

"It seems as if there must be more to it than that. If you know where to look."

"Well, you looked. The dance, OK? Ellen May and all that bunch?"

"You don't have to be nasty about the dance," Sam said.

"Who's nasty? I'm just pointing out. A bunch of phonies. Am I right?"

"Not all of them," Sam said.

"No, but the big shots. Most of those characters are for the birds. And the birds won't have 'em."

"But you have to learn," Sam said. "You have to learn about people, somehow."

"Sam," Mark said seriously, "most of those kids are real, real, real true jerks."

"Eric isn't," Sam said.

"OK. Eric is a good guy. And maybe Roy Johnson, and Debby isn't a bad kid except she runs with the wrong crowd. Even old Thatcher isn't as bad as some, but he needs his head shrunk. He thinks he's God's gift to athletics, and he's not all that good."

She wondered how Mark knew so much when he never went anywhere. Maybe boys just knew more. She would have to start learning. Mentally she wrote in her journal: "I have taken all knowledge to be my province." —Bacon.

ALBERT TOOK SAM AND CORMAC WITH HIM SATURDAY
when he went to meet Aunt Martha at the bus station.
The night was cold and the river was thick black,
in the wake of the boat. The sky, that had been scoured
by an afternoon wind, was now like blue-black velvet
blazing with diamonds.

Albert cut the motor and let the boat drift toward the
dock.

At the scrape of the boat nudging the dock, Sam
tightened her hold on Cormac's collar to keep him from
jumping onto the dock before her father was ready.

Albert tied up, and then said, "All right, boy," and
Cormac made a scrambling leap from the slippery bow
to the dock. He skidded and fell against Albert.

"Cormac," Albert said, "you have all the grace of a
sea cow."

"He slipped, Daddy," Sam said.

"Don't be so defensive about him," Albert said.

"You're just like your mother. Anybody would think I was a monster." He got into the pickup and waited for Sam to put Cormac in the back.

Sam knew she was getting the wake of a scene between her parents. She had heard them talking late the night before, her mother's voice low, her father's rising now and then, and falling abruptly again as if her mother had shushed him. There was uneasiness in the house, and it seemed to come from Uncle Everett's behavior.

It was Saturday night and the town was restless. Men came in from the ranches to search for a little excitement. Their wives went to the movies or wandered through the Mercantile, which stayed open till nine on Saturdays, or went with their men to the bars. The younger boys stood in loose, uneasy knots on the corners or lounged against the pool tables at Big Swede's or drove their cars very fast through town, "peeling rubber" as they swung wildly around corners, yelling for the sake of yelling, whistling and shouting at the girls.

It was triple-feature night and free dishes at the Rialto. Three horror pictures. Sam wished she could go. It would be fun to see what they were like. The posters lining the entrance displayed vampires dripping with blood, a giant automaton come to life with huge metal hands raised for murder, and a slightly-clad girl limp in the arms of a grinning gorilla.

"Culture," Albert said. He was driving slowly past the theater, looking for a parking place.

Sam thought of an old record they had at home, part of a collection that her mother had when she was young. "Saturday Night Is the Loneliest Night in the Week." Maybe that was why people got together and acted crazy, because they were lonely.

Albert swore under his breath and jammed on the brakes as a stripped-down Ford, full of boys roared through an intersection. "That's one way to solve the population explosion." He turned down the street to the high school, and parked. It was a quiet tree-lined street, dark and deserted except for a light in the school building. Sam saw the light and knew that it was the music room.

There was an empty lot stretching from the school grounds to the main street, containing only a public telephone booth, a Lucky Lager billboard, and a litter of trash. Across the street an empty house sagged in the darkness.

Albert locked the pickup and they walked toward Main Street. They turned left, toward the bus station, half a block away. The neon signs of the bars and the filling stations flickered in the yellow half-light of the street. Juke boxes blared and voices rose. Sam shortened Cormac's chain leash.

A man staggered out of a bar and almost collided with them. Cormac growled. The man saw him and backed away in terror.

"Jesus, Mary, and Joseph!" He crossed himself, and flattened against the wall. "It's the werewolf himself."

Albert chuckled, and scratched Cormac's ears. "I wonder if we need a special license for a werewolf."

In front of the bus station Sam looped Cormac's chair around a lamp post and went inside with her father. The station was small and filthy. There were two rows of worn, plastic-covered benches. A man was stretched out, asleep, on one. And from the other, a thin, tired-looking woman made a half-hearted effort to control three small, dirty children, who chased each other noisily around the room. Albert frowned as one of the little boys careened against him.

"Floyd, come here," the woman said. The child paid no attention.

While Albert talked to the man behind the ticket counter, Sam studied the row of dispensing machines along the wall. Soft drinks, cigarettes, dead-looking sandwiches wrapped in waxed paper, gum balls, a juke box. In contrast to the rest of the room, the machines looked shiny and clean. At the end of the room a man in worn ranch clothes leaned against a pin-ball machine, studying it carefully, as if to discover its secret before he risked his dime.

Albert came back, at last. "The bus is late," he said, exasperated. "More than an hour."

"What happened?"

"Broke down." Albert gave the entire station a sweeping glance of scorn. "Stupid, inefficient organization. We talk about exploring space and we can't even get a bus in on time."

"Never mind," Sam said. "It will get here after a while." When they went out, she looked back at the strained face of the woman on the bench. She wondered if she would have to sit there an extra hour.

"We'll have to hang around, I suppose," Albert said. "If it was anyone else, we could go on home and they'd call when they got here. But you know Martha. She has to be met, and right now." He lit a cigarette and looked down the street, frowning.

Sam unhitched Cormac. "Why don't you go and have a beer or a cup of coffee, Dad?" she said. She knew that was what he wanted to do.

He hesitated.

"I noticed the lights on at school. Miss Barracini goes there at night and plays the cello. I'd like to go listen."

"Well," he said, "I don't want you wandering around at night. This town goes crazy on Saturday night."

"Cormac will be with me."

"All right." He walked with her back to the school grounds and stood for a minute at the gate. He tilted his head to hear the cello. Faintly the sounds lifted and faded and came again. "OK," he said. "I'll be at Pete's. Take care of her, Cormac." He walked rapidly up the street, his boot heels crunching on the gravel.

Sam watched the slouching swing of his shoulders until his outline was dissolved in the shadows. Still watching the spot where her father had vanished, she shivered. A little verse that her mother sometimes recited went through her mind: "Life is a vapor and full of woe; man cut a caper and down he go."

The opening notes of the Shostakovich cello concerto throbbed in the quiet night, clear and close. Sam sat down on the top step of the schoolhouse, and Cormac stretched out on the cool flagstones beside her.

She liked the cello. Not just because Miss Barracini played it, but because the sound was so rich and vibrant, almost a thing you could touch. She thought about Mozart and Schubert. She wished that she were gifted.

The music stopped and then began again at the opening. The notes of the main theme were like liquid fire. Sam lost herself in the pure joy of listening.

A car racketed down the street, touching the fringe of her mind with annoyance at the noise. The glare of its headlights caught her for a moment, impaled her in light, and then was gone.

The music stopped again. The cellist tried a passage,

stopped, tried it again. Then the music stopped altogether, and in a moment, she heard the window being closed. She had intended to go in and talk to Miss Barracini, but the emotion of the music was still strong in her and she felt shy about speaking. Hurriedly she pulled Cormac to his feet and went down the steps. She saw the corridor light go on, and the music room light flick out.

Cormac tugged at his leash, asking for a race across the empty field. She understood his urgency. She, too, felt like running through the dark night. There was no one in sight, and the lights of town seemed far away and unreal. She walked him a little way into the big, vacant lot, pointed him away from the street. The ground was spongy with frost; the veneer of firmness gave way under foot.

"You'll get your big, old feet all muddy," she said.

Cormac strained joyfully, aware of the permission in her voice.

She loosened the choke chain and slipped it over his head. "Come back when I call you." He bounded away and raced diagonally across the field. She whistled when he galloped toward the corner of the main street. He circled and ran back to her. As he came close, he veered away again and ran in widening arcs. She sat on the low wall that divided the field from the street and watched him, enjoying the beauty of his bounding run.

She heard the clatter of a car down the street. She called Cormac. He ran toward her, but a startled jack rabbit leaped in front of him and zigzagged away toward the other side of the field. Cormac was after him before Sam could call him back. He went so fast, weaving and circling, that he was out of sight in a second.

The noise of the car diminished. There was the wail of a siren not far away. It was a sound that always made Sam shiver.

She stood up and whistled for Cormac. That crazy dog. A wolfhound, a sight hound, making a fool of himself trying to snuff out a jack rabbit in the dark. She called impatiently. When he didn't come, she walked a little way into the field. "Cormac!" She called and whistled. If he didn't shape up pretty soon about discipline— She was beginning to worry. If he ran into the street on the far side of the field, there were cars. She began to run.

Then, circling fast in his big long stride, he came back. But the rabbit streaked across the road and Cormac went on after him. Sam was angry now. She was not going to take him off the island again until he learned to come when he was told to come.

She could see him, dimly, poking around in the hedge on the other side of the street. She started after him. The car that came racing down the street came fast and without lights, and she never quite realized it was there until she felt the sharp pain in her hip and the sensation of air rushing at her and the world turning on its side. Then she was hurting all over and there were great flashes of lights in her head, and a confusion of sounds. She tried to open her eyes but nausea and dizziness wracked her, and she closed them again. But she had seen the two forms bending over her, and she heard their voices as if they came from a long way off. In the distance she heard Cormac baying the rabbit.

The boys were Terry and Axel, and she wanted to speak to them, but she couldn't make her voice work. She lay still because it hurt less that way.

"Is she dead?" It was Terry's voice.

"Of course not. It was just a shove more than anything; we didn't hit her head on or anything. She's just knocked out. Let's blow."

"We can't just leave her here," Terry said. "She may be hurt bad."

"She's breathing," Axel said. "Look, we can't let that cop catch us here. I mean, speeding, no lights, and now this. Come on!"

Sam tried to open her eyes, to speak, but she couldn't do it.

"There's a light in the school," Terry said. "I'm going to call the school. I'll disguise my voice. We can't just leave her here."

"All right, all right." Axel's voice was rough with worry.

Sam felt hands pulling her to the side of the road. There was a sharp pain in her arm. She moaned.

"Here comes that dog!" Terry's hands let go of her shoulders, and she cried out in gasps of pain. She heard the boys run, and the car start up and roar off. Then she felt Cormac's nose nuzzling her face. She tried to tell him to go to the scholhouse, but the effort was more than she could manage. The world inside her skull spun very fast and her ears roared unbearably.

When she was aware of things again, it was in flashes. Time and place telescoped, became meaningless. Faces and voices came and went abruptly. Miss Barracini. Her father. Dr. Johnson. The sheriff, who kept trying to ask her something. She knew it was the sheriff because he had made a speech to the assembly about careful driving.

When she could finally keep her eyes open, she was

in a strange room. She was in bed, and Miss Barracini and Dr. Johnson and her father were looking at her.

"Where's Cormac?" Sam said. "Where's Aunt Martha?"

"Cormac's in the kitchen, eating as usual." Her father smiled at her but he looked pale. "Aunt Martha is waiting in the car. She was too upset and tired to come in."

She tried to sit up but Dr. Johnson gently pushed her down. "Easy does it," he said. He always said that. Whether she had mumps, or strep throat, or broke her shoulder when a mare threw her, he always said, "Easy does it."

She looked down at her arm. The wrist was in splints and bandages. Vaguely she remembered opening her eyes and seeing Dr. Johnson bandaging her wrist. It had hurt, but it didn't hurt now.

"I guess I got banged up," she said. She touched her head. It was bandaged.

Her father leaned toward her tensely. "Sam, do you know who it was? Who hit you?"

Sam closed her eyes. "Some car, I guess."

"Let her be," Dr. Johnson said.

"But the sheriff wants to know," Albert said. "*I* want to know." He sounded fierce.

"I said, 'let her be.'" It was Dr. Johnson's stern voice.

Albert sounded angry. "The sheriff has his job to do . . ."

"And I have mine," said Dr. Johnson. "You go on home now and mind you don't scare Babe to death. Tell her Sam is *all right*. She just needs a little rest."

"I'll look after her, Mr. Daley." It was Miss Barracini's voice, soft and kind.

"Thank you, very much. You are very good to us."

Sam felt her father's light kiss on her cheek. "Rest easy, baby. We'll see you in the morning."

"Here, cowboy," said Dr. Johnson. "Take this." He had called her that since she was a little girl. She took the pill and drank some water. The motion made her head spin.

"Good girl. Now you get some sleep."

"Sam," Miss Barracini said gently, "if you wake up and want anything, I'll be in the next room. Just call me."

"Thank you," Sam murmured. And she felt the first floating sensation of a relaxed sleep.

Later, she awoke with a jerk. Her head ached and she felt stiff all over. For a moment she didn't know where she was. The first faint lifting of the dark that was not quite dawn gave the room a dreamlike look. She put out her hand and touched the cool tile top of a table. There was a glass on it. She curled her hand around the glass, comforted by its solidity.

Slowly the events of the evening came back. She lay still, thinking about Axel and Terry. They shouldn't have been driving like that, fast and without lights. They shouldn't have left her. But, she knew they had been scared.

The door opened softly and Miss Barracini came in.

"Hi," Sam said.

"Hi." Miss Barracini smiled down at her. "How do you feel?"

"Pretty good."

Miss Barracini pulled up a little arm chair and sat beside the bed.

"Who found me?" Sam asked.

"I did. Cormac came running up to me when I left the school. He took me to you."

"No one called the school?"

"The phone was ringing when I came out, but I didn't go back to answer it. Why, Sam?"

"Nothing," Sam said. "I just wondered if whoever hit me might have tried to send someone . . ." She let her voice trail off.

"Try not to think about it now."

"Could you stay a minute or two?" Sam felt shivery and anxious.

"Of course." She settled back in the chair. "I've been reading poetry—Walter de la Mare. Would you like to hear one?"

"Yes."

Miss Barracini recited the lines softly, like a lullaby.

"*Slowly, silently, now the moon*
  Walks the night in her silver shoon;
  This way, and that, she peers, and sees
  Silver fruit upon silver trees;
  One by one the casements catch
  Her beams beneath the silvery thatch;
  Couched in his kennel, like a log,
  With paws of silver sleeps the dog;
  From their shadowy cote the white breasts peep
  Of doves in a silver-feathered sleep;
  A harvest mouse goes scampering by,
  With silver claws, and silver eye;
  And moveless fish in the water gleam,
  By silver reeds in a silver stream."

Her voice trailed off, and smiling, Sam fell asleep.

BABE STOOD IN THE DOORWAY OF MISS BARRACINI'S SUN-splashed living room and blinked. The room glowed with color; scarlet and blue Navajo rugs, blue draperies, brightly-colored book jackets and record albums, many vivid pillows, a tall vase of chrysanthemums; and, in a cage by the south window, a golden canary sang.

Sam said, "Hi, Mom." She grinned and moved stiffly toward her mother. Babe gasped. There was a bandage around Sam's forehead, her face was scratched, and her wrist was in a cast.

"Sam!"

"I'm OK," Sam said. "I just look terrible."

Miss Barracini held out her hand to Babe. "I'm Angela Barracini," she said. "She really feels better than she looks."

Sam watched her mother shift her gaze to Miss Barracini, and she noticed her look of surprise.

"How pretty you are," Babe said.

Miss Barracini laughed. "Thank you. Please sit down. I have some coffee all made." She was wearing green Bermuda capris and a lemon-colored shirt and leather sandals. She did not look in the least like a schoolteacher, Sam thought.

Babe looked at Sam again. "My husband didn't prepare me for all this."

"He probably didn't want to worry you," Miss Barracini said. "I'll see if I can get your husband and the doctor in here for coffee. Please make yourself comfortable."

She went to the door. "Doctor, you and Mr. Daley had better join us."

The doctor and Albert came into the room. Her father, Sam noticed, towered over everyone.

"I'm getting the coffee," Miss Barracini said. She started out of the room.

"I can't stay, Angela," the doctor said. "Give me a rain check."

Miss Barracini went out of the room.

"The doctor says she can go home," Albert said to Babe.

"But keep her in bed until I see her again," the doctor said. "That was a nasty crack on the head."

"Is she all right?" Babe said. "I mean is there anything I should worry about?"

The doctor laughed and patted Babe's arm affectionately. "If I know you, you'll find something. But there's nothing *I'm* worried about, as long as she does as she's told."

"I will," Sam said.

"All right. I'll see you in a week." He called goodbye to Miss Barracini and went out with his brisk walk.

Miss Barracini came in carrying a silver tray with a steaming coffee pot and four cups.

Albert took the tray from Miss Barracini and put it down on the table.

Miss Barracini opened the swinging door again and Cormac padded into the room. Sam started up but Miss Barracini held out her hand. "No, it's all right. I let him in. He looked so lonesome in the truck."

"Cormac," Sam said. He came to her and lay down at her feet.

"He's a magnificent dog," Miss Barracini said. "You ought to show him, Sam."

"I want to," Sam said eagerly. "Do you really think he's good?"

"He looks great to me. I'm no expert but I've seen quite a few Irish at the Westminster show. We'll have to ask Mr. Stone. He used to raise golden retrievers, you know."

"I've been training him for obedience," Sam said. "He does pretty well."

Miss Barracini held out her hand to Cormac. He sniffed it tentatively. "He looks good enough to me to show for conformation. He's almost grown, isn't he?"

"A little over ten months," Sam said.

"Then you could start him off in the puppy class. We'll have to find out when the shows are. Mr. Stone gets the *American Kennel Club Gazette*. I'll ask him."

In spite of the pain in her head and in her wrist, Sam felt a great glow of happiness. She could see her dreamed-of life coming closer and closer. "What is a dog show like?" she said. "I've tried to imagine it. Is it like a stock show?"

Miss Barracini laughed. "Sort of, I guess. They show

in groups—terrier, hound, sporting, non-sporting, and so on. And there are different classes within groups, according to breed, and then broken down again into owner-raised, owner-bred, American-bred, male, female, and so on. It's a lot of fun."

"Do you really think Cormac is good enough?" Babe said. "It must be awfully disappointing to think you have a good dog, and find out you haven't.

"He's good," Albert said. "I looked into McDermott's kennel record. He raises a lot of champions."

"Could I enter him the next time there's a show?" Sam was almost afraid to ask.

"We'll see," her father said. He got up and put down his coffee cup. "I think we'd better be getting you home. Thank Miss Barracini for her kindness."

Sam thanked her, and Babe added, "Indeed we do thank you. I don't know what would have happened if it hadn't been for you."

Warmly Miss Barracini took her hand. "I'm glad I happened to be around."

On the way home the motion of the pickup made Sam's head pound, but she closed her eyes and thought about dog shows and her friend Miss Barracini.

I<small>T WAS</small> S<small>AM'S FIRST DAY OUT OF THE HOUSE EXCEPT FOR A</small> couple of brief visits to Cormac in the barn. Today she was allowed to take Cormac for a short walk in the woods. The air was sharp and the wind flung itself into their faces in angry little gusts. She was surprised to find how quickly she got tired.

"Never spend time in bed," she told Cormac. He trotted close beside her. She laughed aloud at the idea of Cormac in bed, like Red Riding Hood's wolf.

During her stay in bed her father had brought home all the library books he could find on dog training and dog raising. "If you're going to do it," he told her, "you might as well do it right." And Mr. Stone sent, by Mark, old copies of the *American Kennel Club Gazette*. Babe had become interested, too, and Sam knew that her concern was less for the dog shows themselves than for getting Sam "out into the world." But Sam welcomed all help, regardless of motives. She was almost afraid to admit it even to herself, but after careful study of the prize-winning Irish, it seemed to her that Cormac looked very good.

She looked down at him appraisingly as they came up the meadow path to the barn. Head long, frontal bones of forehead slightly raised, very little indentation between eyes. Skull not too broad. Muzzle long and somewhat pointed. Ears small. Neck long, strong, well-arched, no dewlap. Deep chest. Long back. Long and slightly curved tail. Strong, straight legs.

"Your feet might be too big," she said, "but perhaps you'll grow into them. I grew into mine."

They went into the warm barn. It felt good to get out of the wind. She still had the cumbersome cast on her arm, and the cold made her wrist ache.

She went into the tack room and got a halter that she was braiding with horsehair. If she stayed in the barn another half hour or so, she would miss having dinner with the family. Aunt Martha was getting on her nerves. She kept making roundabout references to the accident and to the criminal character of hit-and-run drivers. Sam could tell that her parents had told Aunt Martha not to ask questions, but she might as well; she talked all around it.

The subject had come up directly only once. Her father had come up to her bedroom and said that the sheriff wanted to know if she knew who it was that hit her. She could tell that her father wanted her to say. But she had spent a long time thinking about it. If it had been only Axel, she might have told. But she couldn't do it to Terry. He hadn't wanted to leave her there, and it was almost certainly he who had called the school. If she told, his life might be ruined. She couldn't bring herself to do it. But she wasn't sure she was right. Everything that had to do with people was so complicated.

She looked at her watch. It was almost dinner time, but her mother would save some for her. Her mother seemed to know when to leave her alone, when to join her in pouring over the dog books, and above all what questions to leave unasked.

She shifted Cormac's head out of her lap so she could get hold of the halter that she was working on. Her fingers were free of the cast, but it was difficult to use them.

"As soon as I can," she told him, "I'm going to quit school and concentrate on you. We're going to build the best Irish wolfhound kennel in the country. We'll call it the Cormac Kennel, OK?"

Cormac gave her a lazy slurp with his tongue.

"Aak!" She wiped her chin on her sleeve, feeling the hard plaster of the cast underneath it. She wished she could get out of the stupid cast. It slowed her down, made her awkward. But she knew from the way her wrist ached that it would be a while yet.

Mark came into the barn. "Mom wants you."

When she got to the house, her mother met her at the door, her eyes shining. "Sam! There's a dog show in Polson December 2nd!"

Sam gasped. "How do you know?"

"Mr. Stone sent you the new *AKC Gazette*. He marked it. Look, it's right here."

Sam peered over her shoulder at the little boxed item that Mr. Stone had neatly marked off. "All-breed show," it said, "Polson, Montana, December 2." Sam's heart began to pound.

"We must send for the application blank right away," Babe said. She was almost as excited as Sam.

"Can I go?" Mark asked.

"We'll all go. This is going to be a great day for this family." Babe hugged Sam.

"Where is this we're all going?" Albert came into the kitchen. He looked wary, and Sam had a terrible feeling that he was going to say they couldn't go, after all.

Mark showed him the Gazette. "Old Cormac is going to be a big fat world's champion," Mark said, but he grinned at Sam and she knew he was pleased, too. Anxiously she watched her father's face.

He frowned, studying the item. "It won't be the big glamorous deal you think," he said. "Dog shows are full of crummy people out to cut each other's throats."

But he had not said no, and Sam relaxed.

"We'll watch out for the crooks," she said

She ran upstairs to her room before he could say anything more. She got out her journal and opened it to a blank page. Holding the pen awkwardly with the tips of her fingers, and resting the cast on the page, she printed carefully: *On the second of December of this year Miss Sam Daley will exhibit her magnificent Irish wolfhound, Cormac, at the Polson AKC dog show. Cormac is expected to win everything in sight. A new era of excellence will open in the dog world.*

She read the words over and over. Then she got out all her dog books and curled up on her bed.

Her first day back at school was surprising. She still had the cast on her arm, and although the bandage had been taken off her head some days before, there was a long red scar from her hairline to the outer edge of her eyebrow.

She had grown accustomed to these things, but at school she was a sensation. People stopped to ask her how she felt. Her teachers were considerate and kind, and fellow students who had never noticed her before now smiled and spoke to her. She felt a little ridiculous, as if she were flying under false colors.

Then when Terry smiled nervously and asked her how she was, she realized what had brought her all this attention. The word had gone out, she felt sure, that she had not squealed on Terry and Axel. She was being rewarded for something she was not sure she was proud of.

She tried to put the whole thing out of her mind, but it was difficult, since she was constantly being reminded.

When Debby said hello to her, she forestalled the questions about her health. "Are you going to take your dog to the Polson show?" she asked.

"I might," Debby said. "If I can get the family car. She never wins anything, but I like to show her for the fun of it. Are you going to take yours?"

"Yes," Sam said. She tried to say it calmly but it wasn't easy. She felt like yelling it.

"That's great," Debby said. "He's a beautiful dog. Lots of luck."

"Thank you," Sam said. The bell rang. She watched Debby hurry off down the corridor. She liked Debby very much. A girl who went to dog shows had to be a really nice person.

She popped into the music room between classes to tell Miss Barracini.

"Wonderful!" Miss Barracini said. "I'll get Mr. Stone to take me. We'll cheer you on from the sidelines."

For a minute Sam was overcome with self-consciousness at the idea of Miss Barracini watching her.

As she was leaving Miss Barracini's office, Terry caught up with her again, alone this time. It was almost time for the bell, and the halls were nearly empty. "Listen," he said in a low voice, "I really am sorry about your accident."

"That's OK," Sam said. "I'm fine now." She didn't want to be late for assembly. And she didn't know what to say to Terry.

"I heard you had a fractured skull." He hurried along beside her.

"No, just a concussion."

"Just a concussion." He looked as if he were going to cry. "People have died from concussions."

"Well, I didn't," Sam said.

At the assembly door, as he opened it for her, he said, in a voice so low she could hardly hear him, "Did you tell the cops who did it? I mean do you know who did it?"

Sam felt chilled. He was only worrying about his own skin. "I didn't tell anybody anything," she said.

His face cleared. "Boy, that's a break! For whoever it was, I mean."

"Yes," Sam said. "I suppose it is." She went on into the assembly hall just as the principal began to lead the pledge of allegiance.

During the announcements she felt herself being watched. She turned her head and met Axel's eyes. He looked away quickly.

Later in the afternoon Sam was summoned to the principal's office. Mr. James looked at her with what she knew was meant to be kindness. He was a small, bullet-headed man with a reputation for being tough. It was hard for him to take the fatherly approach. But he tried.

"Sam," he said, "sit down. How are you feeling?"

"Fine," she said. "Very good, really."

"Splendid," he said.

Sam wondered sometimes whether anybody except teachers and characters in nineteenth century novels ever said "splendid."

"I know you want to put all this unpleasant business behind you . . ."

"Yes," she said.

"But your father and the sheriff have spoken to me." Oh no, Sam thought. How could he?

"I understand that you have not felt sure enough of the drivers of the car to identify them."

"No," Sam said.

"Do you think they might have been boys in this school?"

Sam looked out the window. Some boys were whacking a tether ball.

"I don't know," she said. She hated lying. She hadn't really had time to think through the question of whether or not it was ever defensible.

"You see," Mr. James went on, trying hard to be patient, "this was a serious thing, a criminal thing."

"I know," Sam said.

"If you could identify these boys, they could be put away where they belong." He looked at her hard.

"That wouldn't help them much, would it?" Sam said. "I mean even if I knew."

He tightened his mouth. "The purpose of punishment is to protect society, not do good to the criminals."

"I'm not really sure I believe in that," Sam said.

"Well," he said sarcastically, "until you manage to get your own social and penal code into effect, I'm afraid we must abide by the laws that we have."

Sam sighed. "I'm sorry I can't help you, Mr. James."

He bent over some papers on his desk. "You may go."

She knew he was very angry with her. She hated to have people angry with her. But she had made up her mind.

After school while she was waiting in the yard for Mark, she saw Axel walking toward his car. He slowed down and then turned back and came over to her. He stopped in front of her, his face deadpan. "I heard old James was pumping you," he said, "about the accident."

"What of it?" she said.

142

"What did you tell him?"

"What difference does it make to you?" Sam felt suddenly very angry. He was trying to bully her.

"I just happen to be curious," Axel said. "Just curious, baby." He stepped closer, almost threatening.

"I know why you're curious," she said, "and don't call me 'baby.' "

"Why am I curious, baby?"

"Because you're not very anxious to go to prison," Sam said. She had never meant to confront either of them with the fact that she knew who the drivers had been, but she was too mad to care now.

He looked startled. "You better not be saying wild things like that," he said.

"You know they aren't wild."

"You start telling anything wild like that and you'll get into trouble."

"You scare me." She started to go past him. Mark was coming toward her.

Axel grabbed her by the shoulder. "I mean it, kid. You open your mouth and you'll regret it."

Sam jerked loose from his hand. Mark came up behind them and spun Axel around. For a moment Sam was frightened. Mark was lighter than Axel. But he was pretty good at judo. He had learned it from a book.

"Stay away from my sister," he said.

Axel laughed. "Get lost, junior."

Mark didn't move.

"I said get lost. Go back to nursery school." He reached out his big hand to shove Mark, but Mark ducked, and flipped him off his feet with a shoulder throw. Axel fell hard on his back. He struggled to his feet. Again Mark threw him. This time the wind was knocked out of Axel, and he lay on the ground, his legs twitching.

"Come on," Mark said to Sam.

"Is he OK?"

"Sure. Just got the air knocked out of him."

They walked down to the boat landing in silence. Then Sam said, "Thanks, Mark."

He grinned. "It was nothing. If you need any help any time, just call on old Lancelot. I keep my sword and shield always at the ready."

Sam wanted to tell him that it was a great thing to have such a brother. But he was already spinning the starting rope on the outboard, and the engine sputtered and clattered into life.

When she was in her room, she got out her journal and wrote, "The Soul selects her own Society—Then—shuts the Door."—E. Dickinson.

On the day of the dog show at Polson, Sam awoke before it was light. She got up and looked out the window. There was a very light snow falling. For a moment she was dismayed. What if it snowed too much to drive to Polson? But when she opened the window wider and put her head out, she saw that there was not likely to be much on the ground for awhile. She crouched by the window for a few minutes, feeling the soft touch of the snow on her face. She flexed her wrist, out of the cast now but stiff.

She got dressed and went out to the barn to get Cormac. On the way she had terrible fears. What if something were wrong with him? What if he had broken loose and run away, looking for wolves or something? What if he were sick?

She ran the last few yards, her boots sending up little puffs of snow behind her. Cormac was in his stall, just waking up. She hugged him.

"I thought you might have died or something," she said. She leaned back and looked at him. "You look fine." She got the brush and scrubbed his sides with it until he pulled away in protest. "OK," she said, "but you have to look your best. This is the day."

She took him with her to the house. Her mother was already in the kitchen, frying bacon. "I was scared when I saw the snow," Babe said.

"Me too," Sam said. "But it isn't anything."

"Call your father and Mark, will you, dear?" She patted Cormac.

"I was so afraid something might have happened to Cormac," Sam said.

Her mother glanced at her quickly. "If it had, it wouldn't be any worse today than any other day."

"What do you mean?"

"I mean we love him just as much whether he's going to be in a dog show or not."

"Sure," Sam said. She wasn't sure what her mother was getting at. But there wasn't time to puzzle over it.

During breakfast Albert watched Babe, who was carefully packing fried chicken and bread and butter sandwiches in aluminum foil. "What on earth are you doing?" he asked.

"I read somewhere," Babe said, "that people at dog shows eat fried chicken for lunch."

Albert groaned. "Spare me. It's not enough that a man has to be herded out of his bed at dawn to drive fifty miles in the snow—he also has to eat cold fried chicken!"

"I thought you loved fried chicken," Sam said.

"Not cold, and not at a dog show. I intend to have lunch at the Salish Hotel. And I may be dreaming, but I expect my wife to come with me."

Babe laughed. "All right. But I'll put up lunches for the children. Sam can't leave Cormac, after all."

It seemed to Sam a very long time before everyone had finished breakfast and was ready to go. Aunt Martha was still asleep; she had declined the pleasure of the dog show. They went out quietly, locking the door.

When they got to the other side of the river, Sam was pleased to find that her father had already put clean straw in the back of the pickup, and the tarp over the top. She tried to thank him but he hustled her into the back, with Cormac. The snow was coming down steadily now, and he was anxious to be off. Mark and Babe sat in front.

Sam stretched out on the straw beside Cormac. "You've got to look impressive," she told him. "Very dignified and slightly fierce. Only for heaven's sake, don't bite the judge when he sticks his hand in your mouth. He's only looking at your teeth. And don't get mad when he pokes at your bony structure."

She had entered him in four categories—puppy class, American-bred dog, novice, and open dog classes. Until this moment it had not really seemed possible to her that he would not win all four and go on to best of hound group. But now she began to think that it was, after all, quite conceivable that he would not place. There were Mr. McDermott's dogs to consider; and probably other people in Montana and the general area might have very good Irish. "You might be competing with some of your brothers and sisters," she told him. "You mustn't feel bad, Cormac, if you don't win them all. After all, this is our first try."

She lay comfortably on the straw, half dozing. At last she felt the pickup slow down, stop and start, and turn corners. "We must be in Polson." She sat up and began to brush Cormac again. He groaned in mild protest but he lay still while she brushed. "Remember," she told him, "you've got a lovely gait. Just remember that."

The pickup stopped, and in a moment Mark unsnapped the tarp. "All ashore that's going ashore," he said breezily.

Sam wished her father and her brother would take all this more seriously. They didn't seem to understand that it was a turning point in her life. Stiffly she climbed out of the pickup and snapped on Cormac's leash. She felt in her pocket to make sure her entrance papers were there.

"Here we go," she said. And she marched off across the fair grounds to the big exhibition hall, without waiting for her family.

As she got close to the hall, she became aware of more and more dogs. All kinds of dogs. From her careful study of the dog books and the Gazettes, she recognized most of them. Foxhounds, harriers, Irish setters, Weimaraners, a pair of basenjis, a German short-haired pointer, Scotties, Welsh terriers, all kinds and sizes and shapes of dogs. Some of them were barking and prancing around on their short leashes, but most of them looked cool and quite at home. It was, Sam thought, the most exciting moment of her life. As she went into the auditorium, stopping to have her papers checked, she thought, "This is it. This is the life for me."

Someone showed here where the hound group was quartered, and she led Cormac down the crowded aisles until she found her place. She boosted Cormac into the stall, and tied his leash. She sat down beside him. The whole huge room was full of dogs; with sight, sound, smell, they assailed the senses. People and dogs pushed up and down the rows, the people carrying cups of coffee or cigarettes, hailing old acquaintances, the dogs pulling back or barking or following quietly, according to their temperament. Sam felt as if she were breathing in the essence of dog.

On one side of Cormac, a disdainful Afghan watched the proceedings, staring haughtily down his aristocratic nose. He didn't even look aside when Cormac hung his head over the dividing boards to see who was there. On the other side there were three Irish wolfhounds lying cozily together, muzzles across each other's necks.

Sam looked at them. Competition. She moved closer to look at the kennel name. McDermott. She looked around for Mr. McDermott but he was not in sight. The dogs were two males and a bitch. One of the males looked like a young dog. She looked them over very carefully. They were good dogs, all right. They were all a kind of pearly gray, not white like Cormac. They looked like the dog she had seen that day on the island. She began to worry. They were very good dogs. Of course they were lying down, and she couldn't be sure how they would look standing up. And whether they would have Cormac's fine gait.

She moved up the aisle, pushing her way past people in folding wooden chairs. There were two more Irish, in separate stalls, with different kennel names. Hogan Kennel and Leprechaun Kennel. There was a young male in the Hogan stall. He looked pretty good, but, Sam thought, not as good as Cormac. He seemed a little short in the body. The Leprechaun dog was older. He looked good too, but too much dewlap. She backed up, squinting at him critically. A fat woman in tight slacks pushed past her and sat down in the camp chair in front of the

Leprechaun dog.

"Is he yours?" Sam asked.

The woman gave her a quick look, sizing her up as a possible customer. "Yes," she said. "You interested in Irish?"

"I have one," Sam said. She nodded toward Cormac. "Just beyond the McDermott dogs."

The woman gave a quick disdainful glance. "Oh, that one."

"He's a pretty good dog," Sam said.

The woman laughed. She had four gold teeth near the front. "Dearie," she said, "I hope you haven't entered him in anything but the puppy class. For your own sake."

"Oh, yes," Sam said. "He's in four classes."

The woman shook her head. "Kids will take a chance on anything."

"What do you mean?" Sam said.

"My O'Hara here has a row of ribbons as long as your arm." She pointed to several blue ribbons tacked to the stall. "Those are only his latest. He's been in all the California shows, from Sacramento to San Diego."

"Well, that's nice," Sam said. "He looks like a fine dog. Except for the dewlap."

"Dewlap!" The woman half got up from her chair, and Sam backed away, bumping into a man with a Great Dane.

"I'm sorry," Sam said, to both the man and the Dane. Without looking back at the Leprechaun woman, she went back to Cormac. Her family was there.

"I'm off to a good start," she said. "I just made a woman mad. A woman with an Irish."

"That's my child," Albert said. "What did you do—

offer to teach her the fine points of showing Irish?"

"No," Sam said, "but she was bragging about all the ribbons her dog won in California. And I said he was a fine-looking dog except for the dewlap. And it's the truth."

"Oh, Sam," her mother said. "That wasn't nice."

"Well, it was true," Sam said.

"Did she ask your opinion?" Albert said.

"No."

"Never volunteer unpleasant truths. The woman might turn out to be a judge."

"She can't be. She's exhibiting."

"Never mind what she turns out to be," Babe said sharply. "Just mind your manners."

A man with a Pomeranian in his arms bumped Albert's elbow. "Sorry," he said.

Albert nodded curtly. "I'm clearing out of here," he said to Babe. "Too many people, too many dogs."

"Aren't you going to watch Cormac?" Sam said.

"You can tell me all about it." To Babe he said, "Coming?"

"No," she said. "You go to the Salish, or wherever you want to go. I'll meet you for lunch."

"The Salish lobby at twelve," Albert said. He left, picking his way fastidiously through the crowd.

Mark came back from a tour around the benches. "Boy, they've got some really wild dogs here. Crazy. There's something called a Puli. You can't tell which end is which. And a Lhasa Apso, this big." He measured a few inches with his hands. "Looks like a white powder puff. Cormac, you look like a real normal dog, except you're bigger than anybody else." He patted Cormac's head.

"He looks as if he'd been going to dog shows all his life," Babe said. "He's more relaxed than any of us."

"I just hope he doesn't get too relaxed," Sam said.

"Debby Frye is over there with her dog," Mark said. "He's a miserable-looking mutt."

"Oh, Mark," Babe said. "Why can't you say nice things?"

"Well, Debby looks good." Mark grinned. "I got to go look around some more."

"You go too, Sam," Babe said. "I'll watch Cormac."

"OK. I have to find out when the puppy class is. And I want to watch some handlers. I'm probably doing everything wrong."

Her mother smiled at her. "Don't be nervous. I'm sure you're going to do just fine, dear."

The PA system was announcing novice Scotch terriers in ring three. Sam followed some people who were leading Scotties. On the way she stopped and checked with the information booth, and found that Irish wolfhound puppies would show at ten o'clock.

She found ring three and sat down on the floor to watch how it was done. There were eleven Scotties. The ring steward tied armbands with numbers on them around the arms of the exhibitors, and the judge started the dogs circling the ring. Sam watched closely. It was different, of course, with a dog like a Scottie; they moved so slowly compared to a big dog like Cormac. One of the things she had been working on was matching her stride to his, and it wasn't easy.

She watched one young boy who seemed to be new at handling. He was making some mistakes, and she wanted to learn what they were so she wouldn't make them. He was nervous, and he kept making wrong turns.

He wasn't listening closely enough to the judge. Remember, Sam told herself, don't get nervous; listen to the judge; watch his motions.

She noticed that when the dogs stood for inspection, the experienced handlers arranged them so their best features showed. One dog was slightly undershot, and the handler kept his head turned so that it hardly showed until the judge looked at their mouths. Some of the dogs barked a lot, but that didn't seem to bother anybody. She tried to pick the winners, but she had them all wrong. One little brindle whom she had thought was great didn't even place.

She noticed that the judge built up the suspense just before he picked the winners. She'd like to be a judge someday.

She walked around watching the different groups being judged. She stayed a long time at the ring where the Danes were. They were close to Cormac's size, and she studied the way the handlers ran with them, keeping them at a fast trot and not letting them break into a run. She wasn't sure that she could change Cormac from a trot to a walk and back again as fast as the judge seemed to expect it.

On her way back to Cormac's stall she ran into Debby, who was walking her dog. Mark was right: it was not much of a dog.

"Hi," Debby said. She saw Sam's appraising glance at the dog. "I know, she's a mess. But I love her. She never wins a thing." She patted the dog lovingly.

"Well, that doesn't matter," Sam said. "She looks very sweet." She leaned over, but the dog's ruff went up and it growled.

"One-girl dog," Debby said. She jerked up on the

leash. "Behave yourself, Gretchen. It's a friend."

Gretchen stopped growling, but she eyed Sam suspiciously.

"Some of the other kids are coming over this afternoon," Debby said.

"Oh, are they?" Sam wanted to ask who, but she didn't. "Miss Barracini and Mr. Stone are coming, too."

Debby laughed. "Big deal. Well, luck with your dog."

Sam went back to Cormac's bench. Mark was there, eating a hot dog. And her mother was saying, "Mark, after I fried all that chicken!"

"Oh, I'll eat that too," he said. "Hey, Sam, did you watch the Dobermans?"

"No," Sam said. She began brushing Cormac.

"They really move! They tuck in their rear ends and those hind legs just drive like pistons. They're neat."

Sam felt jealous of Mark's praise of another breed. It seemed disloyal to Cormac. She unhitched Cormac's leash. "I'm going to run him around outside for a few minutes." She took him through the crowd to a side entrance.

When she went back, she stopped just inside the door to watch a white standard poodle being groomed. He stood motionless on a raised platform with a ring that held his head still. His owner was dusting chalk into his coat and brushing it out again. He was a handsome, intelligent-looking dog. He had an English saddle clip. Sam looked him over carefully, smiling at the pompon on his tail, the bracelets of curly hair on his feet, the topknot.

The woman glanced up and smiled at Sam.

"He's beautiful," Sam said.

"Thank you. You have a fine dog, too."

"Thank you!" Sam felt very warm. Dog people *were* nice.

Before she knew it, the PA system was calling for Irish wolfhound puppies. Sam gasped a stricken good-bye to her mother, and pushed her way toward the ring. She was terrified that she wouldn't get there in time.

There were no other dogs in the ring. Had she misunderstood? Then she saw Mr. McDermott over at the other side. He waved to her and held up his hand with thumb and forefinger circled. She went into the ring. The steward tied the armband around her arm. Sam was glad she didn't have the cast on any more. Even so, her hand was stiff, and she held Cormac's leash in a tense hold that made her hand ache. She looked around for the other dogs. There weren't any.

The judge came into the ring. He was rather an old man, with thin white hair. He looked at his schedule, and glanced up at her impersonally.

"Take him around at a walk," he said.

"Aren't the others coming?" Sam said.

"There aren't any others," he said impatiently. "Walk your dog."

"Come on," she said in a low voice to Cormac. They began the circling walk of the ring, but she felt cheated. What would it mean to show him? How could he help winning, if there was no competition?

"Trot your dog," the man said. And she realized that he had signaled to her to trot Cormac, and she had missed the signal. Pay attention, she told herself fiercely. Pretend there are twenty dogs. She ran beside Cormac, matching her pace to his. At one point he almost broke into a run but she jerked on the leash and he slowed down. He slowed too much and for a moment they were out of step. Then they got into the rhythm again.

The judge signaled her to stand.

She held her breath while the judge ran his hands over Cormac's bones. She had made her family do this, so Cormac would get used to it, but they were familiar; this was a stranger. Cormac looked up at her once, as if questioning the propriety of this behavior. She nodded at him, and he stood patiently.

When the judge opened his jaws, Cormac pulled his head back. "Stand!" Sam said. The judge tried again, and it was all right.

"Run him around the ring once more," he said.

She ran him. Questions rocketed through her mind in time with her step. Why once more? What was wrong? Then he turned abruptly away from her and began writing things on a piece of paper at the table.

Sam didn't know what to do. Did you keep on running your dog when nobody was looking? He hadn't said to stop. She slowed down uncertainly. Then she caught Mr. McDermott's eye. He made a flat downward gesture with his hands, and she guessed he meant to stand still. She stood. Her heart was pounding so hard she thought her chest would burst.

After what seemed a very long time, the judge came over to her and handed her a white ribbon. "Pretty good dog," he said. And he turned away before she could even say thank you. The steward hustled her out of the ring, as four beagles started in.

She stood outside the ring with the ribbon in her hand. She had no idea what had happened. Then Mr. McDermott and her mother and Mark came up to her all at once. Her mother was glowing with excitement. She hugged Cormac. "Good old Cormac!" she said.

"But I got a white ribbon," Sam said. "That's no good." She was ready to cry. If they couldn't win something when there wasn't even any competition . . .

"That's a first place ribbon," Mr. McDermott said, in his slurred speech. "Look at it."

"It's white," Sam said. But she looked at it, and it said "First."

"Winners aren't always blue," Mr. McDermott said. "It depends on the show."

Sam felt a little better. "But why weren't there any other dogs? How could we lose?"

"Sure you could lose. If the judge didn't like him, he could give him anything—second, third, fourth, or nothing."

"We really won?" Sam couldn't believe it.

"For Pete's sake," Mark said, "does it have to be spelled out in the sky?"

"Mark," Babe said.

"You did a nice job of handling," Mr. McDermott said. "You looked very good."

"Thank you." Sam sighed. She felt as if she were floating. "I think I'd better go sit down somewhere."

"We'll see you later. I'm showing against you in novice." Mr. McDermott waved and walked off.

In the stall Sam lay down beside Cormac. She was exhausted.

"Is your head all right?" her mother asked anxiously.

"It's fine." It wasn't, though. It was pounding. But she would take some aspirin when her mother wasn't looking.

"We were so proud of you," Babe said.

"You looked like you were doing a tribal dance in there," Mark said. But he gave her a warm grin.

Sam closed her eyes and tried to blot everything out of her mind for a few minutes, so her head would stop aching.

The novice class was scheduled for eleven thirty, but the show was running a little late. Sam was at ringside at eleven twenty-five. The boxers were still in the ring. To keep her mind off her nervousness, she watched them intently. This time, the one she mentally picked got first. She didn't know anything about the boxer standard, but this dog was a clean-muscled, beautiful creature, with a long rhythmic gait.

"A beautiful dog," Mr. McDermott said.

Sam hadn't realized that he was standing beside her. "Yes," she said, "he certainly is." She looked at the gray wolfhound who was standing near Mr. McDermott. A boy in his teens was holding the leash. "Isn't that your dog?"

"Yes," he said. "That's mine. I don't handle them any more. Got a touch of arthritis."

"Oh, I'm sorry," Sam said

"It's hard to get a good handler," Mr. McDermott said, "but Bobby does pretty well."

The fat woman whom Sam had talked to earlier came up to the ring with her dog. Sam tried to smile at her to make up for her former rudeness, but the woman ignored her. Mr. McDermott noticed and winked at Sam.

There were two other dogs waiting. Sam looked them over carefully. In her opinion, her only real competition was Mr. McDermott's dog. But she knew she could be wrong.

She was right. The same man who had judged Cormach hurried them along, to make up for lost time. Fairly quickly he lined them up and eliminated from first place all but Cormac and the McDermott dog. He had them run around the ring again. Sam noticed that Mr. McDermott's Bobby did not pace the dog evenly.

There was a long, tense pause while the judge examined both dogs a second time. Cormac pulled away again from the man's touch, and the man was annoyed. "You've got to teach that dog to stand," he said.

"Cormac, stand!" Sam said. She was so nervous, her voice squeaked.

The judge backed away and looked at them. Then he pointed to Cormac for first, the McDermott dog second, the fat woman third, and dismissed the others.

It was always over so fast at the end that Sam was a little dazed. When she came out of the ring, Mr. McDermott shook her hand. "Very good, very good."

"I'm sorry," Sam said. "I mean I'm glad but I'm sorry about your dog."

Mr. McDermott chuckled. "That's all right, lass. Cormac reflects glory on McDermott."

Everyone broke for lunch then, some of them taking their dogs outside, others milling around, talking in groups. There were smells of coffee and hot dogs and the sizzling smoke of frying hamburgers. And her mother was right. Sam noticed; many people were unwrapping cold fried chicken.

Mark came back to the bench, his hands and pockets full of samples of dog food. "Hey," he said, "it's free. You can get enough stuff to feed old Cormac for at least a day."

"Mark," Babe said, "should you have taken all that?"

"Sure, that's what it's for."

Babe looked at her watch. "I have to go find your father." She was reluctant to leave.

"Aren't dog shows marvelous?" Sam said.

Babe smiled. "They are."

"Especially when you win," Mark said. He rubbed Cormac's ears.

"They're fun anyway," Babe said. "It isn't important about winning."

Sam looked up and saw Miss Barracini coming toward them. Pleased, she jumped up.

"Sam, you were wonderful!"

"How nice to see you." Babe seemed really pleased. "Have some fried chicken. We have enough for the whole show."

"Just a little piece," Miss Barracini said. "Stone is getting us some hot dogs. If he can tear himself away from the hunting dogs. He's having the time of his life."

"I didn't know you were here," Sam said.

"We arrived just in time to see you win. We ran into Debby Frye and Terry Thatcher. They said you won in the puppy group, too."

"Against heavy competition," Mark said.

Babe explained that she had to leave, and in a moment Miss Barracini spotted Mr. Stone in the crowd. "Good luck in the other groups," she said. "We'll be watching. You handle him very well, Sam."

And then they were all gone. Mark too, on some exploration of his own. Sam huddled up in the corner of the bench beside Cormac and tried to relax.

In the afternoon the tension began to build. You could feel it everywhere. Owners and handlers were grumbling about the judges' decisions, some were arguing with each other. People sat around the rings watching in tight silence.

At two o'clock Sam and Cormac went into the ring again for the American dog competition. Sam was beginning to feel more confident. She sensed that Cormac was enjoying it, too. He responded readily to commands. "You're a big show-off," she said to him fondly.

All the dogs except for the California woman's belonged to the McDermott kennel or were from McDermott litters. There were seven dogs. Again Cormac got the nod for first place, and three of Mr. McDermott's dogs took the other ribbons. The California woman announced loudly that the judge was prejudiced and she was not going to show any more at these hick operations.

Half an hour later the open dog showing was ready to go. This time Mr. McDermott had two dogs of his own, and a rancher from Libby was showing two dogs from the McDermott line.

"You're descended from a very good bunch of people," she told Cormac. "No wonder you're winning." He lay down on her feet. "Up, Cormac. Come on." She tugged on his leash and got him up, and ran into the ring.

It took the judge a long time to make up his mind. Once Sam looked up, when they were lined up, and saw both her parents and Mark and Miss Barracini and Mr. Stone, watching intently. It made her nervous. Later she saw Debby and Terry Thatcher at the other end of the ring. She wondered why Terry was there. He didn't seem like a dog show type.

This time Cormac stood patiently while the judge examined him. Sam felt very proud of him. He looks so noble, she thought. She wanted to hug him, but you couldn't do that until the judging was finished. She was feeling much more confident now. Still, she felt a shock of surprise when Cormac placed first.

Almost at once the judging of best of breed followed, and again Cormac won. Her family and Miss Barracini and Mr. Stone cheered, and there was some applause around the ring. When Sam came out of the ring, she noticed that even her father looked pleased.

"Sam," Miss Barracini said, "Mr. McDermott says you have enough points to enter the hound group." Her eyes shone.

"That she has," said Mr. McDermott. He came up to Sam, leading two of his own dogs. His eyes were warm with approval. "You've done a fine job, both of you. Now win the hound group for us. Let's show those other hounds what an Irish can do."

Sam was too tired and happy to speak. She just smiled at them all and patted Cormac over and over.

There was about an hour before group judging. Sam took Cormac outside and let him run around. Happy to be released, he ran around her wildly in big circles in the snow. Finally he came back and flopped at her feet, panting, and let her brush the snow from his coat.

The winter sun was low in the sky and there was a thin cold in the air, almost like metal. A westerly wind had come up. Sam breathed deeply, to get the close indoor air out of her lungs. After awhile she found a big rock; she brushed off the snow and sat.

If Cormac should win in the hound group, he would be eligible for best of show! She closed her eyes and let herself imagine Madison Square Garden for a minute. What must it be like? She would have to question Miss Barracini about it.

"Hello."

She opened her eyes with a start. It was Terry

Thatcher smiling down at her. He looked very attractive, in saddle pants and a sheepskin-lined suede coat. She did not want to talk to him.

"Hi," she said.

"Congratulations. You've been going great guns."

"Thanks," she said. "I have a good dog."

He laughed. "There was a time when I didn't think so, but I guess you have, all right." He looked warily at Cormac. "He's a big brute, isn't he?"

"Irish wolfhounds are supposed to be big."

"Yeah. Listen, Sam . . ." He hesitated. "I just wanted to tell you—I mean, you've been nice to me and all—and it just so happens that the man who's going to judge the hound group is my uncle."

"Oh," Sam said. She didn't see any other reply that could be made, except "so what?"

He seemed disappointed. "Well, I thought I'd let you know. Who knows, maybe you'll make best of show."

"Maybe," Sam said. "but I doubt it."

She watched him walk back to the auditorium. Why had he told her that? What did she care who his uncle was?

"Well, come on," she said to Cormac. "Back to work."

Almost everyone in the auditorium seemed to be crowded around the ring where the hound group was to be judged. Sam began to feel nervous, again. She had no way of telling how good the other breeds were. There was a slender, aristocratic Russian wolfhound, that reminded her of Uncle Everett's confusion of the Irish and the Russian; there was a basenji, red with a white blaze and white stockings, beautiful as a tiny deer; there were an afghan, a big, waddly basset, a fawn-colored whippet, a dachshund, and a beagle. For all she knew, they might be fantastically good dogs. She began to worry about losing. Her mother's words came back to her, about its not mattering whether she won. But that was silly; of course it mattered.

The new judge, whom she hadn't seen before, motioned to them to walk around the ring. It was very different, going around with other breeds. What if Cormac had to pace himself to the dachshund and the basset? His gait was one of his great assets. She wished she had been to a dog show before so she would know what to expect.

The judge lined them up for close inspection. Sam prayed that Cormac would hold still. This judge was more smiley than the other one, but not so quick and skillful with his hands, she thought. For a moment she remembered that he was Terry's uncle, and then she forgot it in her concentration.

Cormac stood beautifully. He didn't even glance up at her for reassurance. She gave him a quick hug when the judge went on to the beagle.

Then the judge called them out one at a time and had them pace their dogs up and down the ring. That was a relief. Cormac ran magnificently, as usual. She studied the judge's face, hoping he was impressed, but you couldn't tell what he was thinking.

He took a long time, and she began to realize that this was part of the drama. This was getting close to the big scene, and a smart judge made the most of it. Over and over again, he would pick two or three dogs to examine once more, or to send up and down the ring. You had to watch him closely to know what you were supposed to do.

Then there was the long business of fooling with paper and pencil. Tired, head pounding, Sam wondered if he was really adding up points, or just doodling to build the suspense. She glanced at the crowd around the ring. They were packed in tight, and they were very quiet. She wanted to say to her mother, If you don't think it matters who wins, look at those people.

Then with a dramatic flourish the judge pocketed his paper and pencil, and pointed to the winners. First, the afghan. Second, the beagle. Third, Cormac.

The first person she ran into as she left the ring was Terry Thatcher. "I told you!" he said. "I told you if I spoke to my uncle, you'd get a ribbon. Now we begin to be quits, right?"

She had never wanted quite so much to hit someone right in the face. She pushed past him, and ran Cormac back to the bench, avoiding everybody.

Then they were all there at once—her parents, Mark, Miss Barracini, Mr. Stone, Mr. McDermott. All of them acting as if something great had happened. She felt like screaming.

"What's all the fuss?" she said. "We placed *third*."

Her mother looked distressed. "Sam, third is good."

"Sure," Sam said. She looked away because she was afraid she would burst into tears.

"Let's go," her father said. "It's getting dark."

"Oh, Albert," Babe said. "I want to see who gets Best in Show."

Albert raised his hands in despair. "My whole family has gone insane."

"I'm ready to go," Mark said. "I'm up to here in dogs."

"Listen," said Mr. Stone, "if Angela wants to stay, your wife and Sam and the dog can ride home with us.

I have a station wagon."

Sam didn't want to see the rest of the show but she was ashamed to say so.

"OK," Albert said, "if they want to stay."

"We'll meet you at Finnegan's Last Chance," Babe said. "If it isn't too much trouble for Mr. Stone." He shook his head. "You and Mark go and have some hamburgers. We won't be late."

Albert shrugged, and he and Mark left.

Mr. McDermott moved in and stood with one booted foot on the edge of the bench. "You're disappointed, little girl," he said gently.

Sam looked up at him. "I could die."

"But that's all wrong . . ." Babe said, worried.

Mr. McDermott smiled. "It's the way of dog people, ma'am. Your daughter is dog people, through and through. She handled that hound like a champion."

Relieved that someone understood, Sam smiled at him. "Thank you."

"And the dog. He's very good." He grinned. "I'll buy him back any time at twice the price."

"Oh," Sam said, "don't ever tell my father that!"

They all laughed. Sam felt much better.

"Listen," Mr. Stone said, "after they choose the best in show, let's all go to the Salish and have some supper. Personally I'm starved."

"Good idea," Miss Barracini said. "Will you, Mrs. Daley?"

"Of course," Babe said.

"You too, Mr. McDermott," Mr. Stone said.

"A pleasure," said Mr. McDermott. "And I have some business to discuss with Miss Sam."

IN THE COFFEE SHOP AT THE SALISH, THEY SAT AROUND
discussing the merits of the best-in-show winner, the
afghan. None of them, except Mr. McDermott, had seen
an afghan before, and he was explaining to them that
this was probably one of the oldest pure breeds in the
world.

"Sam ought to take Cormac to the Westminster
show," Miss Barracini said. "Don't you think, Mr. Mc-
Dermott?"

"I think it would be very nice," Mr. McDermott
said, in his slow, careful way. He finished his coffee and
lit his pipe.

"New York?" Babe said. "Oh, her father would
never allow it. Besides, it's expensive."

"That's what I was thinking of discussing with the
young lady," Mr. McDermott said.

Sam held her breath. She had no idea what he was
going to say.

"I have a dog I'd like to show at Westminster, but I need a good handler." He looked steadily at Sam. "The young lady did very well in the ring. Very well indeed."

"There you are," Miss Barracini said. "No problems. You show Mr. McDermott's dog, and Cormac; Mr. McDermott pays your handler's fees; I'll even go along as chaperone."

"If you aren't serious," Babe said, "don't get her hopes up."

"I'm serious," Miss Barracini said. "Are you, Mr. McDermott?"

"I never joke about my dogs," he said.

"But I have to go to school." Sam felt dazed.

"You could miss a couple of days. We both could. We could fly." Miss Barracini was shining with delight. "I would *adore* a few days in New York. February, isn't it?"

Mr. McDermott nodded.

Sam said, "Wait. You mean I would show your dog and Cormac, in Madison Square Garden?"

"Right."

Sam felt faint. "I can't believe it."

"I don't know what her father will say," Babe said.

Miss Barracini laughed. "We'll gang up on him. I adore overcoming obstacles."

"But you don't know my husband," Babe said.

Sam only half heard the rest of the conversation. She sat there eating her Denver sandwich and drinking her milk in a state of abstraction. She was not in Polson; she was in New York. She was showing Cormac before thousands of people, competing against hundreds of dogs.

In one remote part of her mind she heard the trend of the conversation change. She half heard that Mr.

Stone had applied for a Fulbright fellowship in New Zealand, and she half heard Mr. McDermott talking about dogs down under.

Someone said something about judges, and suddenly all that Terry Thatcher had said to her flashed into her mind and fell into place. "Mr. McDermott," she said urgently. "Is it ever true that judges are dishonest or unfair?"

He looked surprised. "I'm afraid so. Sometimes. They're human, you know."

Sam felt sick. Maybe what Terry had said was true. She had to find out. "If you had been the judge in the hound group, how would you have rated them?"

He thought for a minute, studying the bowl of his pipe. "Afghan first. Beagle second. Basset third. Cormac fourth."

"Mr. McDermott!" Miss Barracini said. "That's treason."

Mr. McDermott smiled. "I know. But that was a fine basset."

"Excuse me," Sam said. She got up from the table. "I'll be back in a minute." She went out into the lobby. She knew, because it had been announced repeatedly over the PA system, that the judges' dinner was being held at the hotel. She wandered around, looking for judges. Finally she asked the desk and found out what room they were in.

Frightened, she went down the corridor to the banquet room. There were knots of people standing around talking. She saw the man who had judged the wolfhounds, so she knew she was in the right place. A woman with a big badge on her dress asked if she could help her.

"I'm just looking for the man who judged the hound group," Same said. "I was an exhibitor. I just wanted to ask him something."

The woman frowned, but at that moment Sam saw him. She brushed past the woman and went over to him. He happened to be standing alone at that moment, lighting a cigar. He looked at Sam, then smiled in recognition.

"The girl with the Irish wolfhound," he said.

"Yes, sir," Sam said. Now that she was here, her knees were shaking. But it was too late to go away without speaking. "I just wanted to ask you something."

"Ask away."

"Are you Terry Thatcher's uncle?"

He looked surprised. "Well, I didn't expect that question. No, I'm not exactly his uncle. He is some kind of distant relative of my wife's. I know him, of course. Nice boy. Excellent basketball player. Why, if I may ask?"

"Did he speak to you about me? About my dog or anything?"

He frowned, puzzled. "No. I don't think so. Terry is quite a talkative boy, and I must confess I don't always listen closely, but as far as I can remember, no."

"Thank you very much," Sam said. She left the room before he could say anything else. She was not at all sure he was telling the truth. Not at all. And yet it didn't seem likely that a real dog show judge would risk his reputation for a friend of a distant relative of his wife's. The more Sam thought about it, the more unlikely it seemed. She felt better.

In the lobby the others were waiting for her, except Mr. McDermott, who had had to gather up his dogs and go home.

"He said to tell you," Miss Barracini said, "that he was serious about the Westminster show."

When she got home, Sam went directly to bed and fell almost at once into a deep sleep. She woke up later when the house was quiet. She turned on her bedside lamp. It was two A.M. She tried to go back to sleep but she couldn't. She kept thinking about Madison Square Garden. There were a couple of small shows in Helena and Spokane, before February; she could go to those and get some extra points. Even if she didn't win anything at Madison Square, just being there was almost too electrifying to think about. Then she began to think about Terry Thatcher again; it was strange what the accident had done to him. Would he go on being that way? She hoped not. But what would stop him? Did she have to be the one? The thought was disturbing.

Finally she got up and dressed and started for the barn. She could tell from the stirring in her parents' bedroom that her mother heard her. But she would understand. In the barn she curled up beside Cormac and pondered the whole problem again. Was there something to be said for the law after all? She didn't sleep until she had made up her mind.

AT SCHOOL SHE LOOKED FOR TERRY. IT WAS NOT EASY
to get a chance to talk to him alone. He was always surrounded by groups of admiring girls and boys. But
finally she got a chance to tell him she wanted to speak
to him after school. The whole thing made her very
uncomfortable, but she was determined to go through
with her decision.

The newspaper had come out and she found herself
a minor celebrity. There was a picture of Cormac and
her, and a story about his winning best of breed. Quite
a few people congratulated her. It was nicer than the
attention she had received because she had not told
about Axel and Terry. But it won't last, she thought. As
soon as I tell Terry about my decision, it will all be gone
and they will hate me. She was sorry.

Terry was waiting for her in the parking lot. He
looked nervous and he tried to conceal it with bravado.
"Hi ya, Uncle Sam, champion dog girl. What's up?"

"Terry." There was no sense wasting time about it. "You've got to tell the sheriff it was Axel and you."

For a minute she thought he was going to burst into tears. "Why?" he said finally.

"Because it's the law. And because it's better for everybody all around." She knew she didn't sound too great. In fact, she sounded downright stuffy. But she did believe it. Terry would never feel right about things, she was sure, until he told. He would always feel guilty.

"We didn't mean to hit you," he said. "And I did call the school, but nobody answered."

"I know," she said. "That's why it's better if you tell. Because you didn't mean to do wrong so there's no reason not to. I know you didn't want to leave me there. I'll tell the sheriff I heard you say so."

"And if I don't tell, you will," he said. "Is that the deal?"

"I guess it is."

"I don't think we did anything wrong." He was trying to sound tough.

"There's a hit-and-run law. Besides, you wouldn't have told me all that stuff at the dog show if you hadn't felt you'd done something wrong."

"I just wanted to help you out."

"It was like a bribe."

His toughness melted. "Listen, Sam, I might even get tossed into the prison farm."

"I don't think so," she said. "And anyway, we have to do it."

"We," he said bitterly. "I like that." He took a deep breath. "OK, I'll see the sheriff this afternoon."

She walked slowly across the parking lot. She felt awful. Now everybody in school would really hate her.

She almost turned around and ran after Terry to tell him she didn't mean it. But she didn't. Just the same, she wished it hadn't happened to her.

Eric caught up with her. "Hi," he said. "Congratulations about your dog."

"Thank you." She liked Eric and he had stayed her friend, but she didn't feel like talking.

"Want to go for a soda or something?"

"Thank you, but not right now." She looked at him and saw the quick look of hurt. "Ordinarily I'd love to, Eric, but I've got a sort of problem and I'm kind of shook about it."

His face cleared. "Oh. Anything I can help with?"

"You probably could, but I guess I can't talk about it to anybody yet."

"Well, let me know if you need a real swinging solver of problems. I'm your man. Eric the Solver."

He looked very reliable. "How do you feel about law?" she asked him.

"I guess it's here to stay." He looked at her closely. "What do you mean, exactly?"

"Well, sometimes the law seems to me to be awfully harsh. I don't know if punishment really helps people. Do you think it does?"

"I suppose sometimes it does and sometimes it doesn't. Depending on the law and the punishment and the person. But I guess we have to have them. Laws, I mean."

"Because society would fall apart if we didn't."

"Something like that. Besides, some people need to be punished. I mean psychologically. Otherwise they'll feel guilty or something. That's what the psych book says anyway." He grinned. "See? I told you I'd be a big help."

"You really are," Sam said. "Thanks, Eric."

She watched him pick up his bicycle and ride off down the street. She wondered if he knew what she was talking about.

In a car at the curb she saw Miss Barracini and Mr. Stone. They were in very serious conversation. They looked, she thought, angry. They didn't see her, and she was glad.

When she got home, she borrowed Mark's cement-mixer "boat." She didn't even ask him if he minded.

She got her horse and Cormac, hitched the mixer to her saddle with a long rope, and rode through the woods to the river on the west side of the island. The water was faster here, and only frozen in thin film near the banks. She dismounted and wrapped the reins around the saddle horn. The thin ice crackled under her boots as she waded out into the creek. Her boots were water-proof but the water splashed over them and inside, soaking her wool socks. It was shudderingly cold. Cormac and the horse watched her. Cormac tried taking a step on the ice but when his feet broke through, he yelped and jumped back onto the bank.

"I thought Irish wolfhounds were rugged," she said. "Shame on you."

She set the cement mixer upright in the water. The current spun it around and she had trouble holding it. She took off her gloves to get a better grip. The metal was cold and her fingers stuck to it. This was a crazy thing to be doing, but she felt like doing something crazy. Especially something that took up all of her mind.

She got the cement mixer into a little pool of water that was relatively still. She tried to climb in. It was not as easy as she had thought it would be. The thing kept tipping. Finally she managed to get in and sit in a squatting position. Her ski pants were soaked, but the heavy corduroy took a while to soak through. She grabbed a branch of an overhanging dead willow, and broke off a pole. Then she let the mixer float out into the mainstream. It began to spin, and when she tried to control it with the pole, she almost tipped over. The thing was shipping water.

Sam was shivering so violently that it was hard to keep her balance but she was enjoying herself. It was wild. She glanced toward the bank. Cormac and the horse were following along, as she had known they would. She had trained the gelding, when he was still a colt, to stay close by when she felt like walking or swimming or exploring.

The current picked up force and shot her forward. It was breathtaking. She gave up trying to pole around rocks and broken branches. It took all her concentration to stay upright. For a few minutes the forest on both sides of her whipped past. Her cap had blown off and her hair streamed out behind her, soaking wet. Her face glowed with cold and excitement, and Terry Thatcher was forgotten.

Then at a bend in the creek the mixer hit a rock and dumped her into the water. When she got on her feet, struggling to stand up against the fast water, the mixer shot off downstream. There wasn't much chance of getting it. She hoped Mark wouldn't be mad. Maybe when the weather got warmer they could find it. It would probably get hung up somewhere. She made her way cautiously to the bank. Cormac jumped up on her as if he were relieved to see her on firm ground.

"Cut it out," she said. "You'll knock me over. I've got problems enough." She took off her sweater and wrung it out, and did what she could to squeeze the water out of her pants. "Hey," she said to Cormac, "that was fun. But I guess we'd better go home. I'm freezing."

She whistled up her horse and mounted him. The air was sharp with cold, and there was a look of snow in the clouds. By the time they reached the clearing she was shivering so hard she could hardly stay on her horse. It was beginning to get dark.

She slid off the horse's back and turned him toward the path. "Go home," she told him. He gave her an inquiring look and then trotted off down the path. She was too cold to sit on a horse. It would feel better to walk. She ran halfway across the rimed meadow. She thought of Uncle Everett as she passed the spot where she had tended the fire for him. She wished she could build a fire, but the matches that she always carried in her jacket were soaked. Anyway the best thing was to get home and take a hot bath. The wrist that she had broken in the accident was aching like fury. Her parents would probably be angry when they saw her. What she had done was not exactly sensible. But she was glad she had done it. Her mind felt washed out and clean for the first time in days.

She stopped for a moment to catch her breath and to call Cormac, who had taken off after a snowshoe rabbit. He never learns, she thought. A rabbit hound. Ladies and gentlemen of the Westminster Kennel Club, this is my rabbit hound, a real kook. She whistled impatiently. The dark had come down swiftly and the cold was intense. Her teeth were chattering. She heard a swish of wings somewhere over her head but she saw nothing.

" 'And the owl for all his feathers was a-cold,' " she said.

In his own good time Cormac came loping back.

"It's a good thing I didn't enter you in obedience," she said. "You'd flunk the whole thing." She threw a rock for him to chase, in the direction of home. He ran for it, found it, and flopped down on the ground, chewing at it. Sam knew he was tired but he wasn't going to admit it. "You're a big fake," she said. "Come on, move."

He got up and loped along beside her. She looked up and felt wetness on her face. "Look, Cormac. Snow."

Big, wet flakes floated lazily down. It looked like a more business-like storm than the flurry they had on the day of the dog show. It was very late for the first good snow. The Year the Snow Came Late. She had taken to thinking in titles lately. There were no stories to go with them, only the titles. They were a rather comforting way of marking things off.

The snow was coming down harder, and it was difficult to see. She had never felt so cold in her life. Her feet were paining her. She began to run again. She couldn't risk chilblains, not if she were going to be a good dog handler.

About halfway across the meadow Cormac stopped short. She put her hand on his neck and felt the stiffness of his muscles, saw his hackles rise. She put her hand through his collar. "What is it? A rabbit? A fox?" She tried to peer through the curtain of snow but she couldn't see more than a couple of feet. Then she saw a vague shape appear and disappear, melt and solidify and melt. She wasn't sure for a moment that she could trust her own senses. Then she tensed. It was a timber wolf. He was close.

She used both hands to restrain Cormac. He was

pulling hard and growling deep in his throat. She tossed her head to clear her face of snow. In that second she felt the clutch of pure icy fear. There were many wolves —she counted them, four, five—and they were circling around her. In the snow they looked shadowy, but she knew they were quite real.

She tried to keep track of all of them at once. The eerie silence of the snow and the circling figures made her want to bolt for home, but she knew better. She yelled, mostly for the comfort of hearing her own voice. "Go away! Scat! Get out of here." But the snow muffled her voice.

She stood still, holding Cormac back, and trying to think. She figured the distance between where they stood and the edge of the path in the woods that led to home. She tried to think herself into the minds of the wolves. What did they want? They were probably hungry. She shivered.

The circle was narrowing. For a moment she thought of Uncle Everett and how they had laughed at his fear of wolves. It was not so funny after all. But the memory calmed her; she was not going to fall into that kind of panic. She stepped forward toward the woods.

She walked slowly and with great care. Once she slipped, in spite of her caution, and almost fell. Feeling the relaxing of her hold on his collar, Cormac almost broke loose. She clung to the collar as she struggled to regain her balance. "No!" she said. "Stay, Cormac! Heel! You're not going to take on five wolves at once." Unwillingly he fell into step beside her, and she was thankful for the hours of training.

She moved forward again. The wolves who prowled just in front of her, and closer all the time, would either have to scatter or close in when she reached the woods. Dimly in the falling snow she could half sense, half see the dark outlines of the trees. But there was a way to go yet. She thought of a story she had read once about a wedding party in Russia that was overtaken by wolves and devoured. But that was Russia; this was Montana. She had never heard of a wolf around here attacking a human being. She said it aloud to Cormac, and then she said it again.

The nearest wolf crouched close to the ground as he ran around them. He was about twenty feet away now. Sam had to keep mopping her face to wipe away the blinding snowflakes. There was cold snow down the back of her neck and her feet were soaking. The only sound was the slogging of her shoes as she lifted them and the squeak as she put them down again.

The wolves were close enough so that she could see their yellow eyes and broad noses, rather like Cormac's. Their tails streamed out behind them as they loped along. The woods were near now. Sam kept the same pace, although the temptation to run almost overcame her. She felt her breath coming in hard gasps.

Then, without warning, Cormac broke loose from her hold and ran straight for the nearest wolf. Three of the wolves disappeared in the falling snow. The two remaining wolves and Cormac snarled and tangled in the wet darkness. Sam knew she should leave them alone, but she couldn't. She scooped up handfuls of snow and threw them at the thrashing animals. She could not tell wolf from dog.

She moved in closer, and saw blood on the snow. In her mind she heard McDermott's voice saying, ". . . and he will lay down his life to be true to thee."

With a yell she jumped in and grabbed a wolf by the scruff of his neck She was surprised that he was so small. But he twisted savagely in her hands and she couldn't hold him. He jerked loose, tearing open the flesh along her forearm. She saw his teeth bared as he faced her. Then Cormac was upon him, gripping his throat in his powerful jaws. The dog shook the wolf until it went limp. The other wolf was sprawled on the snow, dying, its throat torn open.

In death they looked like harmless dogs. But somewhere near them, invisible, there were three more, very much alive. She grabbed Cormac's collar and pulled him along.

In the woods she slowed down a little. They would be safe now. She was trembling and shivering, and her arm was bleeding. Cormac's fur was torn around the shoulders and chest, and his muzzle had blood on it. She didn't know whether it was his or a wolf's. She kept a tight hold on his collar, and clutched the torn sleeve of her jacket around her arm where it was bleeding. The Year Sam Daley Lived Dangerously. She started to laugh and then checked herself. If she began laughing, she didn't think she would be able to stop.

She saw the light in the barn, and she heard her father come out and call to her. But she couldn't stop. She shoved open the door to the kitchen. Her mother and Mark were there, and they were looking worried. She heard her father come charging up the path. He burst into the house.

"Sam! Where have you been? When I call you, you answer me. . . ."

"Hush," said her mother.

And Sam passed out on the kitchen floor.

SHE HAD A HIGH FEVER. SHE KNEW THAT BECAUSE THEY stood around outside her door whispering about it. They thought she couldn't hear them. She felt terribly hot, but it wasn't too unpleasant. She seemed to be suspended outside her own body. Her senses were so acute that she could hear sounds from the other end of the house. She could hear Aunt Martha breathing as she came up the stairs. She heard doors close as if they were claps of thunder. She wondered if she might be going to die but it seemed like a purely academic question, with no emotion involved except a faint curiosity.

When her family crept into the room, she closed her eyes. She could feel them looking at her. It was ridiculous.

She had very strange dreams, about being a judge at Madison Square Garden and sitting on a throne in red robes, with Cormac sitting beside her the way pharaohs used to be represented on their tombs with their dogs.

And one night she woke up and found the devil sitting in her rocking chair, and they had a long talk about Terry Thatcher. She couldn't remember exactly what had been said but they had argued about the problem of responsibility. He had quoted Scripture, which surprised her. He said things like "Let him who is without sin cast the first stone," and that thing about motes and beams. That was when she suspected his motives, when he quoted the Bible. They had quite a lively philosophical discussion. He wasn't at all frightening, and she was rather sorry when he disappeared in a puff of smoke— not only sorry that he disappeared but that he did it in such a trite manner. She wondered what Ellen May Aronson would say if she told her she had been visited by the devil. Would she get to be Golden Girl then?

And when she opened her eyes again, the doctor was there taking her temperature. He winked at her. There was no point in closing her eyes now. Doctors knew when you were bluffing.

"Sam," he said, "when are you going to quit getting all these things wrong with you?"

She grinned. "I'm fine."

He looked at the thermometer. "Well, you're a whole lot closer to fine than you were." He took her pulse.

Then her mother was there, smiling and anxious.

"Get some nourishment into her," the doctor said to Babe. "Semi-solids. Keep her in bed for another day or so. I'll check with you tomorrow." And to Sam he said, "And whatever it is you do to get into all this trouble, cut it out."

When her mother came back, Sam said, "Hi."

"Hi." She sat on the bed. "Feeling better?"

"I never really felt too bad," Sam said. But she knew her mother thought she was just being brave. "What day is it?"

"Sunday," Babe said.

Sam couldn't believe it. Where had the time gone? "Is Cormac all right?"

Babe nodded. "Your father took him to the vet. He had some minor cuts. He's fine now. But he misses you."

Sam stretched out in the bed. She felt weak and funny. "Is Mark mad because I lost his cement mixer?"

"His what?"

"His boat."

"I don't believe he knows it, but I'm sure he won't be mad." She looked puzzled. "What on earth were you doing in a boat?"

Remembering suddenly why she had been in the boat, Sam sat up. "Has anybody found out who was driving when I was hit?"

"Yes," Babe said. "It was a boy named Thatcher and I don't remember the other boy's name. Thatcher told the sheriff." She watched Sam's face. "You knew, didn't you?"

"What did the sheriff do to them?"

"Booked them, or whatever you call it. There will be a trial. He wants to talk to you."

"Yes," Sam said. "I'll talk to him. It was completely an accident."

"Well, don't think about it now. It will be all right." She put her cool hand on Sam's forehead. "I'll get you some soup."

That evening her father came to see her. He looked uncomfortable, as if he were unaccustomed to sickness.

"It was wolves you ran into, wasn't it," he said, after a few minutes of casual talk. Sam nodded. "I found one of my sheep torn to pieces. I've set traps all around the meadow. When you're well enough to go out, I'll tell you where they are. I found two torn up carcasses, did Cormac do that?"

"Yes," Sam said. "He was terrific."

"He's a great dog," Albert said. "I knew that the minute I laid eyes on him." He looked at her thoughtfully. "I suppose you are serious about wanting to take him to New York?"

"Yes," Sam said.

"You'd hate New York. It's a lousy city."

"Well, I don't suppose I'd see much of it, outside of Madison Square Garden and the hotel." She waited.

He rubbed the top of his head and stretched out his long thin legs. "They've been bringing pressure on me, you know. All those women. It's not easy to ward off a flock of determined women."

"What women?"

"Oh, your mother, and Martha, who doesn't even know what a dog show is but thinks New York is heaven, and your Miss Barracini, who waylays me in the street occasionally to charm me into letting you go. And McDermott's wife."

"I don't even know Mr. McDermott's wife."

"But she knows you. You're famous now. And if you don't go and show McDermott's dogs, he'll show them himself, and she doesn't think he's up to it. Therefore she has a vested interest, so to speak." He dug his pipe and tobacco pouch out of his sagging jacket pockets and filled the pipe.

Men must have invented pipe-smoking, Sam thought,

just so they could prolong suspense in a conversation.

"Well," he said finally, "I don't approve of it, but if McDermott will pay you enough in handler's fees to pay your expenses while you're there, and if Miss Barracini will chaperone you, I'll buy your plane ticket."

"Dad!" Sam slid down in the bed and threw the blanket over her face in ecstasy.

He laughed. "All right. It's your Christmas present. Now go ahead and get well, before I owe my entire substance to the doctor." He stood up. "Mark wants to see you."

Mark came in grinning.

"I'm sorry about your cement mixer," she said.

"It's OK. I found it downstream." He looked at her wonderingly. "That was a nutty thing to do, in ice cold water. I mean, even I'm not that nutty."

"I just felt like it," she said.

He accepted that explanation. "It's been pretty wild around here this week. Doctors, parents, aunts, everybody rushing in and out waiting on you."

She laughed. "You were jealous."

"Naturally. It was all I could do to get a bowl of cold cereal. 'Here, Mark, open a box of shredded wheat.' And I had to do all your chores. Including exercising Cormac. Man, I'm a wreck." He let his tongue loll out of his mouth and panted heavily.

"Have you heard? I get to take Cormac to New York."

"I figured you would. They're so relieved you didn't die. That's a really neat maneuver. If you want something real bad, just get sick unto death and you'll get it."

"Did you think I was going to die?" Sam found it

interesting to think of her considered death, now safely past.

"Nah. I kept telling them you wouldn't. I mean it isn't like you." He looked at her interestedly. "It must have felt funny though. You were really out of your skull there for a while."

Sam felt faintly alarmed. "Did I talk much?"

"Night and day. You never shut up."

"What did I talk about?"

"Oh, gibberish mostly. But a few interesting things."

"Like what?"

"Well, for one thing, it's a good thing old Thatcher went to the sheriff because everybody in this house got an earful about that bit."

"You mean I told?"

"And told and told."

Sam lay still for a few minutes. "What will happen to those kids, do you think?"

Mark shrugged. "Who knows."

"I don't mind so much about Axel, but I hate to think of anything really bad happening to Terry. He's conceited and all, but he's not a bad kid."

"He hit and run, didn't he?"

"He wanted to help me. He argued with Axel."

"Well, if he'd had any guts, he'd have stayed, Axel or no Axel." Mark got up. "I got to go. Some guy in Australia is going to call me on the shortwave. Hey, that's a fabulous place. Do you know what all those crazy words in 'Waltzing Matilda' mean?"

"No."

"I'll tell you later." And he was gone.

During her convalescence, Sam read a lot and thought a lot, but most important, she wrote letters. She wrote to the AKC to get registration blanks for the Madison Square Garden show; she wrote to Mr. McDermott to ask when she could work with his dog; she entered Cormac in two shows that were coming up within a month, one in Helena, one in Spokane. She was determined to be very business-like about the whole thing. She sent away for a book on dog handling, and when it came, she read it over and over. And she wrote to Uncle Everett, telling him all the wonderful results of his gift to her. "Even Dad is impressed," she wrote, "because Mr. McDermott offered to buy back Cormac at twice what you paid for him. Not that I would ever part with him, of course. He is going to be the start of my kennel, and maybe, sort of, my whole life. And I have you to thank, Uncle Ev."

She got Uncle Everett's address from Aunt Martha.

It was a post office box number in Las Vegas.

When the doctor finally agreed that Sam could go back to school, she was both pleased and frightened. Some of the kids had sent her get-well cards—Debby, and Eric, and Hester and Anna and Mary Beth. But they came before the story was out about the accident.

The preliminary hearing had already taken place. Her father had given her the newspaper with the account of the hearing. Axel had denied knowing that he had struck Sam. Terry had told the story as it really happened. The trial in juvenile court was set for March. Both boys were free on bail.

Why do they have to wait so long?" she asked her father.

"Our legal system is not very speedy," he said.

Sam was sure that she would really be ostracized at school now. Terry had probably told everybody that she had threatened him with telling the story.

She walked slowly into the school building, a little shaky, and a little frightened.

But as she walked down the corridor to her locker, she realized that people were speaking to her, more people than had ever spoken to her before. She had become known, anyway. Some were friendly, some looked at her curiously, but there was no open hostility.

She spent most of the day trying to catch up on some of the work she had missed. She talked to teachers about assignments; they were all very kind. Once at a distance she saw Axel. He gave her a quick, malevolent look and disappeared into a classroom. She did not see Terry at all. Debby stopped and asked her if she were going to the Helena dog show. She seemed impressed when Sam told her about New York.

"That's marvelous," she said. "You've got a great dog there, Sam."

Sam stopped at Miss Barracini's office door. Miss Barracini glanced up from her desk and smiled. "Sam, how nice to see you. Come on in."

Sam went in, enjoying the familiar sight and smell of the room. It was good to be back. "I wanted to tell you that my father said it's OK about New York. He'll buy my plane ticket and Mr. McDermott's fee will pay the hotel. So as long as you're still willing to chaperone me, it's all set."

For a moment Miss Barracini had a faraway look. Then she said brightly, "That's marvelous. That's wonderful news. And we'll get you to that dog show, no matter what. Now tell me how you feel."

"Oh, I feel fine," Sam said.

"But a little tired the first day."

"Well, just a little."

Miss Barracini put her hand on Sam's shoulder. "Take it easy. Don't try to get everything caught up all at once."

"I won't." The bell was ringing for English class.

"We'll get together later for a talk," Miss Barracini said, "Oh, and Sam . . ."

Sam turned back. "Yes?"

"I don't know whether you realize it or not, but I think you are rather a heroine around here now."

"Why?"

"Oh, it isn't every girl who wins dog shows and fights off wolves with her bare hands and refuses to 'squeal' on her fellow students even when they run over her."

Sam shook her head. "Those seem like funny reasons

for being a heroine."

"It's a funny world." Miss Barracini turned away to let a boy carrying a cello get into the music room.

Sam walked down the corridor slowly. Once she would have thought it was pretty neat to be a heroine at school, but if it was based on stuff like that, accidents really, it didn't seem to mean much. Still, it was pleasant to have people smiling at her, asking her how she felt.

Just before her last class Eric caught up with her. "Hey, you want to go bike riding with me tomorrow after school? Provided it doesn't snow again."

"I don't know how to ride a bike," Sam said. Then she saw that he thought she was putting him off. "But I guess I could learn. I can't go far though; I'm still wobbly in the knees."

"OK. I'll see you out by the bike rack right after school."

"I don't have a bike," Sam said.

He was hurrying off toward his next class. "I'll bring my sister's. We may skid around some but there's not too much snow."

THE NEXT DAY THERE WAS A HEAVY SLEET STORM SO THE bicycle ride was postponed. It was, Sam thought, just as well, for she still felt low in energy. And she had a great deal of work to do to get caught up in her studies.

Christmas vacation came, and although it was usually Sam's favorite time of the year, she was more interested this year in catching up on school work and in getting Cormac ready for the dog show. She took him out for the prescribed half hour of training every day, and she spent hours brushing his rough coat. She set up mock dog shows with Mark or one of her parents as judges, to get Cormac used to the handling. She didn't want him jerking his head away from a judge again.

Christmas and New Year's were gone, it seemed, in a flash. On the first day of school Eric reminded her of the bike ride. "It's good weather for it, like spring."

It was an exciting day for Sam, for she had in her pocket the completed registration form for the West-

minster show, to show Miss Barracini. But when she went
to find Miss Barracini, she was not in her office. Disappointed, Sam put it off till tomorrow.

She met Eric at the bike rack. "I fall off these things
whenever I try them," she told him.

"You are in the hands of an experienced teacher. I've
taught two sisters and a brother, and no broken bones."

"If I break any more bones or anything," Sam said,
"I think my family will throw me out."

"I was kidding," he said, "We'll take it slow. You'll
be OK."

"All right."

Eric disengaged two bikes from the rack, a girl's and
a boy's. "Here you go. Take it slow now, and if you start
to wobble too much, lean a little and put your foot on
the ground."

"Could we wait till we're out of sight of the school?"
Sam said.

He grinned. "Vanity, vanity. OK. we'll walk to the
corner."

After they had rounded the corner, he stopped. "All
right, I'll steady her while you get on." He propped his
own bike and held the rear fender of hers.

Gingerly she straddled the bike and put one foot on a
pedal.

"I'll give you a little push to get you going."

"A *little* push," she said. "Once my brother gave me
a push on his and I couldn't stop till I hit a tree."

"Quit worrying."

Suddenly Sam found herself moving, weaving wildly.
Eric rode a little behind her, steadying her bike as well
as he could.

"Don't go too slowly," he said. "It's harder that way.

The thing wobbles all over."

Sam began to get the feel of it. "It's kind of like riding a horse," she said breathlessly, "only horses don't tip over."

He pulled alongside her. "I wouldn't know. I never was on a horse but once."

"A Montana boy who never rode a horse?"

"Just once, on a mare that pitched me right on my head after twenty seconds of glorious equestrianship. That was enough. I still have the bump. I always tell people if I'm stupid, it's because a mare creased my cerebellum. Whoops, watch that pothole."

Saw weaved and wobbled wildly, and managed to hit the pothole dead center. It almost threw her out of the saddle.

"Sorry," Eric said, "I shouldn't have mentioned it. One of my sisters is like that; if there's one big rock in a mile of road, she'll hit that rock trying to avoid it."

When Sam got her breath back, she said, "I'll teach you to ride a horse if you want."

"No, thanks. They scare me spitless. When I was little, my grandfather had a horse that used to chase me all over the place, I used to wear this big, old straw hat and that darned horse would chew on it. He scared me to death. Of course I didn't have enough sense just to take off the hat and give it to him."

Sam laughed. And once she started laughing, she found that she couldn't stop. The bike teetered perilously. She glanced at Eric. "I'm not laughing at you," she said, between giggles. "It just struck me funny . . . the hat and the horse . . . because I know how horses are . . ." She came to a wavering stop, one foot on the ground.

Eric bent over his front wheel, punching it to test for air. "Listen," he said, "I'll race you to Gallatin Park."

Sam got back on the bike, swayed perilously, and then took off down the street.

Eric passed her and then stopped at a little grocery store. He motioned her to keep on going. Before she reached the park, he caught up with her, balancing a paper bag on the handlebars.

The park was only a small grove of willows and mountain ash, with a couple of children's swings and a battered picnic table. They left their bikes and walked to the edge of the noisy little creek and sat down. The snow was gone, except in dark patches. The sun was unseasonably warm, and the scent of pine was in the air. Beyond them the mountains reared up, snow-capped.

Ceremoniously Eric opened the paper bag. He had two Cokes, a package of chocolate cookies, and some potato chips. "The banquet is ready, Your Highness," he said.

"It looks like a real swinging banquet," Sam said. She had not realized how hungry she was.

They ate as if they had not seen food for weeks. And then Eric leaned back and lighted a cigarette. "It's kind of a vice of mine," he said. "My father said he'd give me five hundred dollars if I didn't smoke until I was twenty-one, but I never made it. Except for the monetary reward, that seems kind of dumb when you think about it. I mean if you're going to get lung cancer, what's the difference whether you get it before twenty-one or after."

Alarmed, Sam said, "You aren't going to get lung cancer, are you?"

He shrugged. "I don't think so. I've studied a number

of case histories, and it's my conclusion that if you stay under half a pack a day, you're in the clear. But I expect to die young, anyway."

"You do?"

"Sure," he said casually. "It figures."

"Why?"

"I just don't see myself as an old guy. And I think people have premonitions about these things."

"Well, don't die too young," Sam said.

"OK," he said. "Want another cookie?"

"No thanks." Sam sloshed the last of the Coke in the bottle. "What do you think it's like to die?"

"Nothing," he said. "*Nada.* So why do people go ape about it? You die and you're dead. Finis."

"I guess they want to hang onto themselves Although when you're really sick, you don't think much about it. Anyway I didn't."

"It's a funny thing. Most people gripe about their lives. You take my mother. Gripe, gripe, gripe, all day long. Nothing pleases her. But she's terrified of death. Every time it comes out in the paper that something is good for you, like yogurt or wheat germ or honey, my mother can't wait till she gets some. Our house is full to the rafters in health foods. And yet she can't really stand herself. I don't dig people."

"I don't dig anything," Sam said. "I think the whole business is just one confusion after another." They sat still in the sun for a few minutes. "The only thing I feel sure of, or at home in, is taking care of my dog and showing him and all. That's all I ever want to do."

Finally they stirred themselves, got up, threw the trash in the trash can. Eric held on to the Coke bottles. "Four cents," he said with a grin.

On the way back they paused while Eric returned the Coke bottles. Then they went on up the street. "I'll call up my father to come and meet me," Sam said.

"No need. I can row you over. I keep a boat at Snell's landing."

As they came to an intersection, Sam realized that the street leading away from them was Miss Barracini's street. "Would you mind if I stopped at Miss Barracini's for just a minute?" she said. "She's going to chaperone me at the New York dog show. I want to tell her the entrance papers are filled out."

"Sure. I'll wait here."

Sam left the bike with him and walked quickly up the street to the house where Miss Barracini lived. As she came near, Mr. Stone came out. He didn't see her. He got in his station wagon and drove off.

Sam ran up the steps and knocked on the brass knocker. Miss Barracini threw open the door, looking expectant. Then her expression changed to surprise. "Sam, how nice! Come in."

"I can only stay a minute," Sam said. "I don't mean to bother you. But I wanted to show you this." She pulled out the registration form from her pocket and handed it to Miss Barracini.

Miss Barracini looked at it for a long time, with a strange expression.

"Isn't it great?" Sam said. "We're all set. I heard from Mr. McDermott, too. He wants me to show one of his dogs, and he will pay all my expenses in New York." She waited. She began to feel uneasy. "It's great, isn't it," she said again.

Miss Barracini looked up at her. "Sam, sit down a minute."

"Well, Eric is waiting for me," Sam said uncertainly.

"Sit down." When Sam was sitting in the chair underneath the canary cage, Miss Barracini said, "The trouble with plans is, anything can happen to upset them."

"What do you mean?" Sam felt fearful.

Miss Barracini sat down and took a deep breath. "Mr. Stone and I are going to be married."

Sam could hear the ticking of the mantel clock. It sounded loud and fast. It went through her mind that seconds really went by faster than you realized. Married to Mr. Stone? He was a nice man, but married to Miss Barracini? It was like putting together a Vivaldi concerto and a song by Stephen Foster. It was unthinkable. She couldn't think of anything at all to say. Miss Barracini's canary burst into sudden, startling song.

"We've talked about it for a long time," Miss Barracini said. "And I held out for a long time. But he's just got a Fulbright that will take him to New Zealand at the end of the month. And when it came right down to it, I couldn't let him fly off without me."

Sam looked at her. "This month?"

"Yes. I won't be able to go to New York. Sam, please understand. We'll find some way for you to go. I am sorry."

Sam got to her feet. Her face felt stiff. She wasn't sure she could make it move enough to speak. "That's all right," she said. Her voice sounded cracked. "Congratulations and everything." She hurtled toward the door.

"Sam . . ."

When Sam reached the bottom step, she looked back. Miss Barracini had tears in her eyes. It made no sense.

Sam ran all the way back to Eric and the bikes. He gave her a quick glance and asked no questions. In silence they rode to the river and in silence he took her across in his little rowboat. The water was steel-grey and very still.

He helped her out at her boat landing. "It's none of my business," he said, "but my advice is, don't pay too much attention to adults. I mean we really can't count on them in the long run."

She smiled at him brightly. "Thanks for a nice time." As he still stood there, she looked at the water in order to avoid his eyes. "The river will be frozen pretty soon," she said. "Well, so long, Eric." She ran up the path, tears streaming down her face.

It was almost a week before she told her parents that she would not be able to go to New York, after all. They reacted in the opposite way from what she would have expected. Her father said, "You can't expect a pretty girl like Barracini to give up marriage for a dog show." And her mother was outraged at what seemed to her to be a betrayal of Sam.

"We will solve this somehow," she said grimly. But Sam couldn't see how.

And then a few days later, her mother made some phone calls, and when she was finished she was smiling triumphantly.

"The McDermotts will chaperone Sam," she said.

Albert frowned. "We hardly know them."

"We know them well enough," Babe said. "And I am sure they are just as reliable as Miss Barracini."

So she was to go to the dog show after all. It didn't seem quite the same to Sam; she was shy about going with a strange woman. But she was going.

LIKE A REIGNING MONARCH UNCLE EVERETT CAME, LADEN with gifts. He was fatter, and he was tanned, and he was wearing an expensive-looking suit. Aunt Martha gurgled over him, and Babe seemed relieved that he was back. Albert eyed him with a mixture of curiosity and contempt.

"What in God's name have you been up to, Everett?" he demanded more than once.

But Uncle Everett always said, "That can wait. First things first." And he would come up with a new batch of presents from his bottomless suitcases. Sam had a pair of real leather thong sandals, jewelled sunglasses, and a silver bracelet set with turquoise. "Made by them Indians," he told her. Aunt Martha got a new diamond watch and both she and Babe were deluged with perfume and bath oil and powder.

"Keeping clean is going to seem downright sinful," Babe said. "I feel like Cleopatra."

"The best is none too good for my family," Uncle Everett said. And of all the things he said, Sam felt that that was the truest.

He brought a beautiful pair of decanters for Albert. For Mark there was a leather pouch with five shiny silver dollars in it.

After dinner, which was the liveliest meal they had had in a long time, Sam followed Mark out to the barn. He had spread the silver dollars out in a neat row, and he was looking at them thoughtfully.

"What do you think, about Uncle Ev?" she asked him.

He frowned. "I don't really know. Something's wrong."

"How do you mean? He looks great and he seems happy."

"Not happy," Mark said. "Keyed up. He's all revved up."

"Uncle Ev is always keyed up."

"This is different. He's nervous about something. He'll have another heart attack if he isn't careful."

She was always surprised to find that Mark did pay attention to people. "Do you think he's in trouble?" When he didn't answer, she said, "Do you think he's a crook or anything?" She was amazed to hear herself asking such a question. She had not known the idea was in her mind.

"I always thought he was sort of a crook."

"Is gambling crooked?"

"Not in Nevada."

"How can something be crooked in one state and not in another?"

He shrugged. "That's how things are."

"But do *you* think gambling is bad?"

"I could care less."

"But do you?"

"I guess not. It's just a question of what a person wants to do. It just seems silly. I mean you know they'll make a sucker out of you sooner or later; that's how it works. But if you like to be taken, then that's your privilege, I guess. I suppose Las Vegas would be OK, if you liked that kind of stuff."

"It isn't Paris," Sam said.

"Oh, Sam," he said impatiently. "Paris is probably just as bad, one way or another."

"I think the whole stupid business is a mess," she said. She wasn't sure what she meant, exactly. She felt like crying. So Mark wouldn't see her cry, she called Cormac and went out.

New snow crunched pleasantly under her boots, and a brilliant moon lighted up the path. Through the windows of the living room she could see her mother and Aunt Martha talking. Uncle Everett stood behind them, lighting a cigar. Then he left the room.

Sam went into the kitchen and pulled off her heavy boots. She heard her father's electric saw whining away in the workshop. She sat down and began to peel an orange. The sound of the saw stopped and she heard Uncle Everett.

"Albert," he said, his voice high and excited, "you just never saw anything like it."

"And never hope to," Albert said. "The spectacle of people tossing away their hard-earned money right into the waiting pockets of a bunch of hoods has never struck me as appealing."

"No, no," Everett said, "it's not like that at all." His

voice rose a little. "Everybody's having fun. And all it takes to come out ahead is a little system."

"Famous last words," Albert said.

"Look, I ought to know. I been going great guns."

"How did you happen to leave then?"

"I wanted to see Martha and all of you."

"Are you going back?"

"You bet your sweet life," Everett said. "I never had it so good."

"You're going to take Martha, I suppose?"

Uncle Everett dropped his voice. "Well, not just now. But you don't need to bring it up."

"She *is* your wife," Albert said.

"Listen, Al, she'll be taken care of better than she ever dreamed of. And she won't stay on here." And then in a different tone he said, "They got girls in that town you wouldn't believe."

"I'm sure," Albert said. He started the saw again.

He needn't sound so righteous, Sam thought. And it struck her with a shock that in some ways her father and Uncle Everett were alike. What was it exactly? Concern for themselves? She knew she ought to go away and not listen to any more of this conversation, but she didn't move.

Uncle Everett said, "I been wanting to talk to you, Al."

"Oh?" Albert hated to be called 'Al.'

Uncle Everett sounded strained, too cheerful. "Yeah. This fellow in Vegas loaned me some money one night. I'd been going great guns, you see, and he thought I could make a little bundle for both of us."

Albert's voice was cold. "But you lost a little bundle instead. And now the man wants his money back."

"Yeah. Sometimes those Vegas fellows are just a little

203

unreasonable, you know? I mean they're great guys and all but . . ."

"But they want their money back."

"That's it. And I can get it back with no trouble at all. I've really got a system, Albert. You can see I done well." He waited but Albert didn't say anything. "So what I need, see, is a little money, about a thousand, to get me going again. Then everybody gets paid back, with interest." His voice almost achieved the old self-confidence.

"Only a lousy thousand," Albert said.

"You'd get it back with interest," Everett said eagerly. "It's no sweat, Albert, no sweat at all."

"I'll tell you what I'll do, Everett."

"Yeah, Albert?"

"I'll give you back the decanters. You can pawn them."

There was a silence. "Look, Albert," Uncle Everett said, "this is no joking matter."

"I would never joke about a thousand dollars," Albert said. "Maybe you could borrow back the jeweled sunglasses and Mark's silver dollars and the mink stole . . ."

"Albert, you don't understand!"

The anguish in Uncle Everett's voice made Sam feel sick. Her father had no right to be so cruel.

"Sure I understand," Albert was saying. "Santa Claus ran out on his luck. And why did you bring all the presents if you're broke?"

"I bought it before," Everett said. "When things were going good. Look, it would just be a couple of weeks, Albert. I'd give you a note."

"Did you ever think of going back to work?" Albert said.

"There isn't time for that. Look, Albert, I'm not kidding. Those fellows play for keeps."

"Oh, cut it out, Ev. You sound like an old movie."

"But it's true!" He waited a minute. "You're really turning me down?"

"That's the general idea," Albert said. "I'll give you a piece of advice, Everett; nothing is really free in this life."

When Uncle Everett spoke again, the words sounded thin and far away. "OK, Albert. OK."

When Sam heard the workshop door close after Uncle Ev, she went in. Her father looked up. "What is it?"

"I heard you talking to Uncle Everett."

"That kind of comes under the heading of eavesdropping, wouldn't you say?"

"Yes," she said. "You were pretty mean to him. He is in trouble."

"And why is he in trouble?" Her father looked at her sternly.

"His luck ran out."

"And what business did he have, trying to play that kind of luck?"

"I don't know," she said.

"What was he doing there, Sam? Where did he get the money in the first place?"

"Gambling."

"OK. If a man wants to gamble, well and good. But he has to take the tough luck with the good. He can't come crying to other people to bail him out."

"He's scared," she said.

"Maybe the scare will teach him a lesson."

"He's been awfully good to us."

Albert shrugged. "Easy come, easy go."

She knew her father was probably right, but it was Uncle Ev.

"He's our uncle," she said. "He's in trouble."

Albert's eyes were cold. "I don't want to discuss it."

Sam went looking for Uncle Everett. What she was going to do had to be done quickly or she would not be able to go through with it. She found him in the barn looking at Mark's radio equipment. His face was white and strained.

"Hello, Sammy." He sounded absentminded, but he tried to smile at her. He sat down on a low rail of the stall. His plump legs dangled. He looked like Humpty Dumpty. "How's everything going? Been to any carnivas lately?"

"No," Sam said, "there aren't any in the winter."

"That's right. Where I been, it's a carnival every minute. And no winter. Lying alongside one of them big swimming pools . . . That's the life."

Sam pulled her breath in sharply. "Uncle Everett, if you are in bad need of money, I could probably sell Cormac back to Mr. McDermott."

He looked at her in amazement. Then his face began to soften. "Sammy, that's mighty white of you."

Sam's mind was racing. It was really her father, of course, who had paid for Cormac, but Uncle Everett probably didn't know that he had given that money to Aunt Martha. Her father would be furious, and he would say she had sold his property, and he would be right, but she would pay him back. It was the only way she knew of to help Uncle Everett.

"You think he'd buy him back?"

"He said he would. At twice what you paid."

Uncle Everett jumped down off the railing and began to pace up and down on his short legs. "We'll go in town first thing in the morning and you can call him. And Sammy, don't you worry none. I'll get you another dog, soon as my luck changes."

"I don't want another dog," Sam said. If she stopped to think what she was doing, she knew she wouldn't be able to go through with it.

"Then we'll buy this one back and you'll go to New York and win all them ribbons."

Cormac was sitting up in his stall, waiting for Sam's attention. She tried not to look at him. "Just let me tell you this, Uncle Everett. I'm doing this so you can pay off your debt, not gamble some more. You were wrong to tell me you were going to Paris. It was a lie."

"Sammy," he said, "I had Paris on my mind."

She went on relentlessly. "You knew you were going to Las Vegas. You lied to me. And you lie to yourself, Uncle Ev."

"Now hold on." His face flushed.

"If you keep on lying, you'll smash everything for everybody. I'm doing this, about Cormac, because you gave him to me, and you've always been good to us, and you're in trouble. But you've got to promise me to quit gambling, to quit telling lies."

He was angry now. "Listen, after all I done for you."

"Presents aren't enough," she said

A muscle in his cheek was jumping and his voice sounded thick. "Don't you give me a hard time, Sam. It don't agree with me. I got this heart condition. Don't you rile me now."

Sam turned her back on him. She put Cormac in his stall and ran to the house and locked herself in her room.

She lay awake most of the night, going over and over the whole thing in her mind. Aside from her own grief, it seemed wrong to sacrifice Cormac to Uncle Everett's folly. But he would be all right with Mr. McDermott. And she could not bring herself to take back the offer she had made. Uncle Everett was all that her father said he was, stupid, selfish, greedy, untruthful—and yet he was their Uncle Everett and he was in trouble.

A little before dawn she heard stealthy footsteps and the creak of the stairs. She sat up, annoyed. On top of everything else, Uncle Ev was just plain dumb. Did he expect to rout out Mr. McDermott at this hour?

While she was getting dressed, she heard her mother go downstairs. That would create a problem. Well, let Uncle Everett explain where they were going; she was too tired to think of anything. She could hear the hum of voices in the kitchen. Maybe if she stalled a little, her mother would go back to bed and Sam could catch up with Uncle Everett.

When she put her comb away in the drawer, she picked up her Thought Book and flipped it open. It was full of a lot of stuff, all right, she thought. One of the last entries was from "Dover Beach":

. . . for the world, which seems
To lie before us like a land of dreams,
So various, so beautiful, so new,
Hath really neither joy, nor love, nor light,
Nor certitude, nor peace, nor help for pain;
And we are here as on a darkling plain
Swept with confused alarms of struggle and flight,
Where ignorant armies clash by night.

She had been very impressed with it when she wrote it down. It was a beautiful poem, but now it made her vaguely angry. It was too self-pitying, somehow. She snapped the book shut and put it back in the drawer. What did it matter how things seemed, or for that matter how they were; you had to live with them as they came.

The voices downstairs stopped and the back door slammed. Uncle Everett was walking down the path and he carried a suitcase. Sam went downstairs as quietly as she could. She didn't want to wake her father.

Her mother sat at the kitchen table, drinking coffee and crying. "He's gone," she said. She looked small and fierce.

Sam smelled the newly-brewed coffee and it made her feel slightly sick. "How do you mean, gone?" She touched the cold top of the table with her left hand.

"I mean clear gone. Out of our lives. No more Everett."

"He's in trouble," Sam said.

"I know. He's been in and out of trouble all his life. He got in, we got him out. My mother, my aunts, your father, me. But no more." She wiped her eyes and looked at Sam reproachfully. "You were going to sell Cormac for him."

"He needed help."

Babe's cup clattered as she put it down. "But Cormac! He isn't just a *thing*."

"I know that." Sam felt like screaming. She knew what Cormac was.

"He isn't worth it, Sam. Ev isn't worth such a sacrifice."

"Don't!" Sam turned away.

Babe stood up so she could face her. "You've got to face facts. I'm sick of people not facing facts around here."

"Maybe I'm the only one who is," Sam said. She took a deep breath. "I would never have had Cormac at all without him. I owe him something."

Babe's mouth trembled.

"I'm the only one who can help him," Sam said.

"Your father could have."

"But he didn't." She got her coat and pulled on the knee-high cloth-top boots that her father had bought for her at the Army surplus."

"I'll never forgive Everett for doing this to you," Babe said.

Sam sighed. "Yes, you will." She put her hand on her mother's shoulder. "Don't worry. Mr. McDermott is a nice man. I'll try to make a deal with him to buy Cormac back in installments."

Babe was crying. "I'll help you, out of the house money."

"We'll make it. If you want something bad enough, and you make that choice, you can do almost anything." She was touched by her mother's grief over Cormac. She kissed her cheek and tasted the salt tears. She felt older than her mother. "It will be all right."

Then Albert was in the doorway, in his bathrobe, sleepy and annoyed. "What is going on?"

"Nothing," Sam said. "Go back to bed, Dad."

"Why is your mother crying?"

"She had a nightmare. Go to bed, Dad." She knew he didn't believe her, but she knew, too, that he would accept the story to avoid hearing anything unpleasant. She seemed to be looking at her father from a great distance, and she saw him as a frightened man. He's as frightened as Uncle Everett, she thought; that's why we're here on the island. She felt wrenchingly sorry for him.

He turned and went upstairs, and Sam ran out the back door to catch up with Uncle Everett.

In the barn she let Cormac out of the stall. As he bounded up to her, she reached down and hugged him fiercely. "Some day, somehow," she told him, "I'll get you back."

She hurried down the path until she reached the meadow. She leashed Cormac, and in the dim morning light she tried to locate Uncle Everett. She knew his direction because the heels of his foolish Las Vegas boots cut deeply into the snow. After a moment she spotted him halfway across the meadow.

Sam watched him a minute. He was having a hard time making progress in the snow. He didn't see her. She could just let him go, and keep Cormac. She wondered if people in Las Vegas really killed people who owed them money, or if it was just in movies that such things happened. She watched him flounder, fall in the snow, and struggle up again, lifting one leg high, and then the other. He looked absurd and pitiful.

She caught Cormac's head and held it against her side so tightly that he yipped. Then she started after Uncle Everett. Cormac tugged at the leash. "All right, go tell him to wait." She unfastened the leash and Cormac bounded out into the meadow. Sam shouted to Uncle Everett to wait.

He turned, almost losing his balance again. He didn't seem to see or hear Sam. He was staring at the galloping dog streaking toward him. He screamed. Sam yelled again and began to run.

"Wolf!" Uncle Everett's voice was a thin shriek of terror. He tried to run.

Sam shouted for Cormac. He broke his stride and circled back toward her. But Uncle Everett floundered ahead. He looked like a man swimming under water. The treacherous snow and the vainglorious boots trapped him. He stumbled and fell and rose and stumbled forward. Then he threw up his arms and seemed to be jerked upward and suspended in space for a moment. Then, thrashing feebly, he fell on his side.

He lay still. The flung suitcase had broken open and spilled out the mink stole and two clean shirts and the diamond watch.

Sam knelt beside him. He had run into one of Albert's wolf traps. His leg was caught and twisted in the big steel jaws. His face was as white and as still as the snow. Even before she touched him, Sam knew that he was dead.

SAM AND MARK STOOD ON THE PLATFORM OF THE RAILROAD station at Whitefish. Babe and Albert were helping Aunt Martha onto the train, and farther down, where the mail sacks were piled up on the big flat handcar and the shiny tin milk cans were being loaded onto the baggage car, four men strained and lifted the coffin of Uncle Everett onto the train. Albert had brought it earlier in the pickup, the twenty-two miles from the funeral parlor in town to the station here.

"He was so sick of trains," Sam said. One more time for the Missoula-Butte run, Uncle Everett. One more time. She felt weighted down with a sadness that went far beyond Uncle Everett and included every living thing.

Mark looked pale. During the church service Sam was afraid that he was going to faint. But he spoke calmly now. "I don't believe death is such a bad thing. It happens to everything alive."

It wasn't really death that was sad. It was life. Sam watched her father swing Aunt Martha's bag onto the platform of the train. It was all the hopes you had and the way they turned out.

Mark took his eyes away from the train for a moment and watched a magpie flying low on the other side of the tracks. "I'm going back to the pickup," he said, abruptly. He ran off across the tracks before Sam could answer him. He had looked as if he were going to be sick. She wondered if she should follow him. But he would hate that. For the first time in her life she saw Mark as a child. She wished she knew how to comfort him.

The scream of the diesel whistle made her jump. Her father leaped off the train as it began to move. She walked down the platform toward her parents. Her mother's face was white, but she had not cried. At least not so anyone could see her.

Aunt Martha's swollen, tear-stained face appeared for a moment at the window as the train jerked into motion. She didn't wave.

"Will she be all right?" Babe said in a low voice, as if she were asking herself the question.

"She'll be all right." Albert took off his hat and waved it at Martha in a slow, ceremonial wave. "Everett left good insurance. And there's the railroad pension."

"I didn't mean that," Babe said

Albert glanced at her. "She'll be all right."

"Oh, Albert." Babe looked unbearably tired. "You always think things will be all right."

As soon as they got back to the island, Sam changed her clothes and went to look for Mark who had gone off into the woods without bothering to change. She found him at last down by the south bend where he liked to ride the rapids in summer. He was huddled up on the bank in a patch of snow-frosted moss.

Sam sat down beside him. "It's cold," she said. But he didn't answer She looked quickly at his face. He had been crying. She couldn't remember when she had seen him cry since he was a little boy.

"I didn't know Uncle Ev meant that much to you," she said gently.

"I hardly liked him at all," Mark said. "He wanted to kill everything."

She wrapped her long arms around her knees. The ground was very cold. "Why do you feel so bad."

He picked up a twig and slashed at the stiff weeds. "Things keep changing. I guess we're growing up or something. I don't like it."

Sam was silent for a few minutes. Then she sighed and said, "Don't worry. Things change all right, but new things can be nice too."

Slow tears rolled down Mark's face. He didn't bother to hide them. "Uncle Everett is dead. What does it mean to be dead?"

"You told me it was just a rearranging of atoms."

"I don't really know what that *means*, though." He wiped his face with his sleeve. "You'll be going to New York pretty soon."

"Well, but I'm coming back," she said. "It's only for a few days."

"*This* time you'll come back."

Suddenly she saw what he was seeing. "Listen," she said desperately, "we all have to face change, all the time. In psych class the other day we were talking about this case of a Mr. X . . ."

Mark interrupted her impatiently. "I don't care about old Mr. X. I care about *us*."

She sighed. "I guess there's nothing we can do about it."

He jumped to his feet. "Well, I know one thing, I intend to do just as little growing up as I can manage." He looked down at her fiercely. "And if you're smart, you'll stay out of the whole mess, too." He strode off down the snowy path between the trees, making deep hollows with his boots.

"We can't keep out of it, Mark," Sam said softly. He couldn't hear her. "We're people. We're stuck with it."

SAM SAT ON THE EDGE OF THE SWIMMING POOL AND watched Cormac roll in the soft snow. An early February chinook had melted the hard crust, and the day felt like spring.

She had a letter in her pocket for her mother from Aunt Martha. Aunt Martha's letters never said much, just 'all fine here. Miss your marvelous cooking. Love to all.' She was living comfortably on Uncle Everett's insurance, and a younger cousin stayed with her.

Babe wasn't at home. She had gone into town to a meeting of the class mothers of Mark's grade. For a while, she had blamed herself for Everett's death until Dr. Johnson finally got in touch with Uncle Ev's doctor and confirmed his own opinion that Uncle Everett had had several coronaries. "And his blood pressure was way up," Dr. Johnson said. "You could tell that just by looking at him." Aunt Martha now had convinced herself that Everett had quit the railroad because of his heart.

Sam packed a little snow under her shoulders and leaned back. She was tired. She and Cormac had been out in the meadow going through training routines with Mr. McDermott's dog. She was bedded down, now, in the barn. She was a fine dog but not as smart as Cormac. Sam hoped she could do well for Mr. McDermott at Madison Square Garden.

She made a snowball and threw it for Cormac to chase. He looked at it and declined. He was tired, too. He had reached his full size and Sam could no longer show him in puppy classes. He had done well at Helena and Spokane in other classes, but there had not been much competition.

She put her arm around his shoulders. "Wait till we hit New York." She spent a lot of time now reading about New York. It did sound terrifying. But Miss Barracini had told her about a hotel a few blocks from the Garden that allowed dogs. She and the McDermotts were going to stay there.

A long letter had arrived for Sam from Miss Barracini. Of course she was Mrs. Stone now. New Zealand sounded like a very strange country. Sam added it to her list, right after the Tower of Pisa.

After Christmas Terry Thatcher's parents had sent him to a military school in the east. He had sent Sam a postcard. The trial was scheduled for March. It was going to be an eventful year. The sheriff had told her father that Terry would probably get off without any sentence, but he wasn't so sure about Axel. Suspended sentence, maybe. Sam dreaded it. She would have to testify. That was the trouble with making choices; you got stuck with the consequences for the rest of your life.

She looked at her watch. It was almost time to go get

her mother. Sam hoped she had enjoyed the meeting. She still wouldn't wear the mink stole. But maybe some day—

She got up and stirred Cormac. He picked up a willow stick and dropped it at her feet. She picked it up. A willow wand. For a moment she remembered the little girl in the carnival. If that carnival came back this year, Sam would find out about that child, herself. Someone ought to do something.

"Come on," she said to Cormac. "I'll race you to the river."